I0743686

DETECTIVE KAY HUNTER: COLLECTED SHORT STORIES VOLUME 1

RACHEL AMPHLETT

Detective Kay Hunter: Collected Short Stories Volume 1 © 2023 by
Rachel Amphlett

All rights reserved.

No part of this book may be reproduced in any form or by any
electronic or mechanical means, including information storage and
retrieval systems, without written permission from the author, except
for the use of brief quotations in a book review.

This is a work of fiction. While the locations in this book are a mixture
of real and imagined, the characters are totally fictitious. Any
resemblance to actual people living or dead is entirely coincidental.

Discover all of Rachel Amphlett's books here:

DETECTIVE KAY HUNTER: COLLECTED SHORT STORIES VOLUME 1

INTRODUCTION

A brief description about each of the short stories you'll find in this collection follows.

Nowhere to Run

When a series of vicious attacks leaves the local running community in shock and fear, newly qualified detective Kay Hunter is thrust into the middle of a fraught investigation.

Blood on Snow

A suburban housewife is found dead in her garden. There is no weapon, no witnesses, and the only set of footprints belong to her cat.

Probationary detective Kay Hunter and her colleagues

are convinced it's murder – but how can they find a killer when there are no clues?

A Burning Question

When a fire deliberately destroys a boat, nearly killing the occupant, Kay Hunter and her colleagues suspect a serial arsonist is targeting a small community of river dwellers.

With another man dead and people fearing for their lives, Kay is desperate to stop a killer who shows no sign of stopping...

NOWHERE TO RUN

CHAPTER ONE

'You're not going to puke, are you?'

Probationary Detective Constable Kay Hunter clenched her takeaway coffee cup between her fingers and looked at the pitiful sight that lay spreadeagled on the bike path.

A biting early April chill cut across the council-managed park, trees see-sawing back and forth as she peered at the outer cordon of blue-and-white crime scene tape and narrowed her eyes at a cluster of onlookers craning their necks, hungry for details.

A dozen uniformed police officers with grim expressions patrolled the perimeter and demanded formal statements from those who hovered at the fringes despite the early hour.

Kay gritted her teeth and resisted the overwhelming urge to kick the senior detective crouching next to the body at her feet.

Ex-military police, Detective Sergeant Devon Sharp's

reputation and no-nonsense approach to his casework sometimes jarred with the younger officers assigned to him, and Kay had no wish to start her investigative career with Kent Police on the wrong foot.

'No, Sarge,' she managed. 'I'm not. I've seen plenty of dead bodies before. Doesn't mean it doesn't affect me though.'

Weak sunlight broke through the boughs of the beech trees lining the concrete path and cast a tattoo of shadows over the victim's bare legs, one running shoe lying sideways underneath a nearby wooden bench.

The flies were already gathering, their incessant buzzing a white noise beneath the murmured voices of Kay's colleagues.

She concentrated on inhaling the rich aromatic fumes of caffeine laced with two sugars and glared at the older constable who stood opposite her, an ill-disguised smirk across his lips. He coughed and looked away, but not before she saw a grin crease his mouth.

Kay swore under her breath and imagined how satisfying it'd be to dump her coffee over the smug—

'Hunter, take a look at this.'

Her gaze returned to the dead female jogger.

Now the Acting Senior Investigating Officer, Sharp lifted the dead woman's arm, turning it gently between his gloved hands.

Kay placed her coffee cup on the concrete path and then donned gloves and protective overalls before lifting the crime scene tape and squatting next to him.

The victim was dressed in calf-length running tights and a singlet vest top.

Kay had found a baseball cap under a nearby shrub and carefully placed it in a plastic evidence bag.

The baseball cap had likely tumbled from the victim's head the moment her skull had caved in with the force of the blow that had ultimately killed her, according to the forensic pathologist who now hovered beside Sharp, head bowed.

Kay reckoned he was right.

That was how the last victim had been killed.

Sharp pointed to the empty cotton smartphone holder strapped to the woman's upper left arm.

'Just like the last one, Sarge,' she said.

'Indeed.'

He stood and began barking orders to the team, sending the junior constable and his colleagues to walk a perimeter to see if they could find the missing phone.

Kay knew it would be a fruitless task.

The killer had been too clever for that.

The pathologist, Lucas Anderson, nodded to her as he passed, snapping latex gloves from his fingers. 'I'll be in touch once I have a day and time confirmed for the post mortem, Hunter.'

'Thanks.'

As Kay dealt with the questions fired at her by the team and made sure she followed procedure at the crime scene, she noticed a blue van being driven across the park towards them.

It slowed as it neared, and then the engine died and the doors opened.

Two figures in white paper suits climbed from the vehicle, hurried to the back doors, and extracted four metal cases before slamming the doors and making their way up the small incline to where she stood next to the victim.

The crime scene investigators.

Specifically, Hugh Hughes and Amber Holstein.

Hugh managed to look like a geek no matter what he wore, due to his shaggy, brown fringe hanging over his glasses. His height meant that he always appeared to be looking down his nose at people, a trait that had the unfortunate tendency to be confirmed once he opened his mouth.

Amber's long blonde hair was tied back and bagged under a paper hat, but the trainee pathologist still managed to wear her work clothes as if she was walking down a catwalk.

Kay peered down at her own crumpled protective clothing and bit back a sigh.

'Morning!' Hugh chirped as they reached the bike path.

Amber set her case down on the floor next to the victim, rubbed her gloved palms together, then turned her back to Kay. 'The killer's left another one for us then, Devon?'

Kay exhaled slowly as the DS brought the pair up to speed.

'Right, right,' Hugh nodded. 'Well, okay then. Let's take a look at her.'

Kay turned her back and walked a few discreet paces away while the team worked and contemplated the investigation to date – one that had now been made more complicated by the discovery of a second victim.

The first murder had been discovered seven days previously, in a park four miles away.

The second murder was only six days before the town's charity run. Constant pressure would come from both Headquarters and the local district council as she and her colleagues tried to assure the public that the town remained safe, while the media would go wild with speculation.

Kay glanced over her shoulder to see Amber working beside the dead woman, and scowled.

She needed more coffee.

CHAPTER TWO

Kay bit back a yawn and glared at the whiteboard.

A sickly sheen covered its surface, the poor lighting in the incident room lending a green tinge to the black markings on the board.

The clack of fingertips on keyboards, shouted requests for urgent reports and muted telephone conversations created a cacophony within the low-ceilinged space, and she wrinkled her nose at the hours-old stench of instant noodles and energy drinks that lingered in the air.

Her gaze flickered over the map that Sharp had pinned to a corkboard, the two victims' places of work and their homes circled with a red felt-tip pen.

Various points of interest had been identified across the map, including where the two victims had been known to shop regularly, attend a gym, and socialise with friends.

'Let's get on with this, and then you can get yourselves home.'

She turned at the sound of Sharp's familiar ex-military bark, then scurried to find a seat near the front of the gathering officers and turned to a new page in her notebook as he began the briefing.

'We have a positive identification for our victim from this morning. Laura Scott, thirty-two – worked as a dental hygienist at a practice in Bearsted. Her pink top was recognised by another runner who went past the crime scene at a distance and who then spoke to one of the officers on duty at the cordon. Apparently, Tanya Green attends the same gym Laura went to and says that they used to meet for coffee after a Sunday morning Pilates class.' Sharp waited while the assembled officers caught up with their note-taking. 'Understandably, Miss Green was shaken up by Laura's murder but has given us some useful information to get us started.'

'Did she know our other victim, Sarah Anderson, Sarge?'

The words were past Kay's lips before she could stop them, and she felt heat rise to her cheeks as all her colleagues turned to her. 'Sorry, Sarge.'

'Not a problem – I'd rather hear your questions as we go along rather than have you forget something at the end.' Sharp gave a faint smile. 'But I'd prefer it if you gave me a chance to get going first.'

Laughter rippled through the incident room, and Kay lowered her gaze to her notebook.

'In answer to Kay's question, no – Miss Green couldn't confirm if Laura knew Sarah, and hadn't heard of Sarah's name beyond last week's news reports.' Sharp glanced down at his notes before continuing. 'Who's currently going through Sarah Anderson's social media accounts?'

'Me, Sarge.' A detective constable by the name of Bradley Thomas raised his hand. 'Do you want me to take a look at Laura's accounts as well?'

'Please – and let me know if you find anything that suggests they knew each other. Kay, I want you to head over to the gym that Tanya Green mentioned and speak to the manager there. In particular, find out whether Sarah was a member as well. In any event, I want to know if he's received any complaints of harassment from his female clientele from other members of the gym.'

'Will do, Sarge,' said Kay, scribbling a note.

'Uniform have spent the morning interviewing Laura's neighbours and immediate family,' Sharp continued. 'I want a review of those statements, as well as those of her friends and work colleagues – see if there is anything that gives you cause for concern, or whether there's anyone who links her to Sarah Anderson. We'll reconvene tomorrow after the post mortem results are received. Dismissed.'

As the team dispersed back to their desks, PC Simon Higgins wandered over to Kay and handed her another sheaf of paperwork still warm from the photocopier.

'That's the last of the witness statements to add to the ones you've already got,' he said. He glanced over his shoulder to where Sharp was speaking with two more experienced detectives, then turned back to her and lowered his voice. 'Do you think it's a serial killer?'

Kay wrinkled her nose. 'It's a bit too soon to say that.'

'Two women, both joggers, both bashed over the head with a blunt instrument? Got to be connected, haven't they?'

She shrugged, unwilling to concede that the same thought had occurred to her during the briefing. 'Best get the evidence to suggest that before we start assuming anything, Simon. Always safer that way, in case we overlook anything, right?'

'I suppose so. Do you want me to come with you to do that interview at the gym in the morning?'

'That'd be good, thanks.' She smiled, recognising the same eagerness to be involved in an active investigation that she had felt before passing her detective's exams earlier that year. 'Meet in the car park at eight?'

'Okay, great.'

Higgins walked away with a bounce in his step.

Kay turned her attention to the pile of witness statements on the desk beside her, a sad collection of stories and memories of happier times.

'Have you eaten anything today?'

Kay jumped in her seat at the sound of Sharp's voice, knocking the witness statements to the floor, then turned to face him, her face aflame.

'I-I, no. No, I haven't, Sarge.'

Kay bent down and began pulling the paperwork

across the worn carpet, gathered it all together, and placed the documents back on the desk.

When she looked up, Sharp was smiling, not unkindly.

'It's been a long day,' he said. 'And we're going to be busy tomorrow. Go home.'

'Thanks, Sarge.'

CHAPTER THREE

Kay unlocked the communal door to the block of flats on the outskirts of Tonbridge and stepped into a narrow hallway, the aroma of freshly cooked food wafting under the door to the ground-floor flat.

As she climbed the staircase, a television played in her neighbour's home on the next floor, the sound of a car chase and automatic weapons following her along the landing.

After she turned her key in the new lock she'd had fitted the day after moving in a year ago, she flicked on lights as she moved through her flat, threw her bag onto a threadbare sofa that was too comfortable to replace, and kicked off her shoes under an occasional table in front of it. Stretching her arms above her head and letting out an enormous yawn, Kay wandered into the bedroom and eyed the running shoes beside the wardrobe door.

The walls shook with another movie explosion.

It was all the motivation she needed.

Throwing her suit trousers and shirt into the washing basket next to the door, she pulled on her running kit before heading back into the living room, placed her phone into the armband around her left bicep and tucked her keys into her sweatshirt pocket.

In two minutes, she was outside and easing into her training route around Tonbridge's northern suburbs, some of the frustration from the investigation disappearing as she broke into long strides.

Following Higham Lane, she headed towards the Hadlow Road and the sound of diminishing commuter traffic. She fell into an easy pace, following the training regime she'd set herself.

The charity run was one she had been looking forward to, a means to ease herself into running longer distances after a knee injury had put her out of action for most of the early part of the year.

It had been painful enough hobbling around at work, let alone trying to exercise when she got home.

Now though, she approached the T-junction and set her sights on the busy main road ahead, pausing a moment to check for oncoming traffic before hightailing it across to the pavement on the opposite side.

Her lungs were tightening now, and she forced herself to slow a little, to relax into a rhythm and breathe easily. This was a regular route for her, a shortened one compared to the elongated run she'd undertaken two nights ago.

Several of her colleagues were planning to run in the charity event, and she had no wish to embarrass herself in front of them.

Especially Amber Holstein.

A truck rumbled past her in the opposite direction, a motorbike following in its wake. In the distance, a police siren rang out from the other side of town and sent a shiver down her spine.

An uneasiness had gripped her since leaving the housing estate where she lived, and now she realised what had been bothering her.

Where she would normally see one or two familiar faces on her route, there was no-one out exercising.

She passed a solitary dog-walker with a black Labrador, the animal being gently berated as it took a distinct interest in a hedgerow, but that was it.

There were no other joggers in sight.

Not a single runner passed her.

A prickle of fear crept across her shoulders, and she picked up her pace as she reached the next junction.

She entered the winding road that snaked through the suburb and headed for home, her trainers pounding the pavement in a steady beat that matched her heart rate.

How were they going to stop a killer who was terrorising the community and had people fearing for their lives?

Ten minutes later, out of breath, she paused at the bottom of the staircase as the door to the ground floor flat opened and a woman in her early twenties peered out, dark eyes sparkling.

'I thought it might be you. Mum sent over too much food as usual – do you want some?'

Kay let out a relieved sigh. 'You're a star, Jasmina. I wouldn't say no, thanks. I haven't had a chance to get to the supermarket this week yet.'

Her neighbour's face clouded before she stood to one side to let Kay in, then closed the door. 'Are you working on that murder investigation? The two joggers?'

'Yeah.' She raised her gaze to the ceiling as loud footfalls crossed the flat above before a door slammed. 'Thank God he works night shifts.'

Jasmina laughed, holding out a Tupperware box. 'Nothing wrong with a Bruce Willis film now and again.'

'Now and again being the operative words. Thanks for this – I thought something smelled good earlier.'

'Honestly, I'd rather have had a pizza, but you know Mum. She worries I might be starving. Do you fancy catching up for a drink later this week?'

'I'd love to, if I can. When does your shift at the surgery finish this week?'

'Six, usually, but I'll get an early finish on Friday.'

'Not catching up with Peter for dinner?'

'He's going out with the football team after practice.' Jasmina wrinkled her nose. 'There's only so much chat about the Premier League I can take.'

Kay laughed as she wandered back to the door. 'Then yes, let's try to get out for a drink.'

'Give me a call once you know what's happening at work.'

'Will do.' Kay crossed to the staircase. 'Thanks again for this.'

'No problem. And, Kay?'

She paused on the first step. 'Yes?'

'Be careful out there, all right?'

The next morning, Kay peered through the passenger window as the pool car passed through Maidstone town centre, her gaze tracing the steady lines of commuters hurrying from the bus stops and train stations towards their places of work.

Beside her, Higgins rested his hands on the steering wheel while his fingers tapped along to a song he hummed under his breath, before he eased into a right-hand turn and pointed at a sign fixed to a lamp post.

'The gym's up here on the left. Do you know this one?'

'No – I cancelled my gym membership after Easter.' She sighed. 'It was getting too expensive, and I was hardly there. I tend to run these days.'

Higgins glanced across at her, then back to the road. 'I heard someone say you were into your running. Are you training for the charity race this weekend?'

'I'm trying to, in between working on this

investigation.' She shuffled in her seat to face him. 'I went for a run last night when I got home. It was weird – there was hardly anyone else around. Blokes, yes – but no women. There are usually three or four who run at the same time as me in the evenings who I always say hello to.'

'These murders have them all spooked,' he said, his lip curling. 'The sooner we find out who's responsible...'

'Still think it's the same person?'

'That's my gut feel.'

'Me too. But, why? What's the connection between the two of them? There's been nothing to suggest they knew each other from the witness statements I've read.'

Higgins turned into a small car park beside a low-slung building and ratcheted the handbrake before pointing to the sign above the double doors. 'I don't know, but I guess we start here.'

McDowell's gym was a privately-owned establishment in one of the more affluent suburbs of the town, its front windows adorned with posters showing smiling models on stationary bikes, lifting weights or posing on rowing machines.

Kay scowled at the pictures as she passed, wondering if anyone in real life ever resembled one of the models after a sixty-minute spin class, and led the way through the doors into the reception area.

A stocky man in his forties with broad shoulders and closely-cropped brown hair looked up from a computer, then frowned as he realised he wouldn't be signing up two new members that morning.

'Dean McDowell,' he said, rising to his feet and shoving his hands in the pockets of his faded jeans. 'Can I help you?'

She noted the logo emblazoned across the front of his T-shirt. 'Are you the owner?'

'That's right.'

After holding up her warrant card and making the introductions, Kay leaned on the counter and gestured to the computer. 'We were wondering if you could confirm that Laura Scott was a member here.'

'Hang on,' he said and jabbed at the keys while squinting at the screen. 'Yes. Joined a couple of years ago, but doesn't attend many classes apart from Pilates by the look of it. I think she and a mate of hers use the sauna a couple of times a week, and I've seen her using the weights room at weekends.'

'That friend of hers––'

'Tanya Green, according to this log.'

'Right, thanks.' Kay tapped her fingers on the counter. 'What about Sarah Anderson – did she come here?'

McDowell clicked through his database, then shook his head. 'No-one here by that name. She was murdered too, wasn't she? Do you think they knew each other?'

'Too early to say, Mr McDowell. We're simply trying to establish known facts at the present time.'

Higgins cleared his throat, and she glanced across to where he stood next to a corkboard. He jerked his thumb over his shoulder at a poster that lifted in the breeze from the air conditioning vent above his head.

Kay recognised the logo for the charity run, then turned back to McDowell.

'Do you know how many members of your gym might be training for that?' she said.

He shrugged. 'Half a dozen, maybe. There might be more – some people don't like to broadcast their training goals in case they don't achieve them, or change their minds.'

'Could you let me have a list of the members you know are planning to run?'

His eyes widened. 'Do you think they're in danger?'

'It's just a precaution,' said Kay. 'We'd like to speak with them, so if you have phone numbers and email addresses as well, I'd appreciate it.'

'Sure.' McDowell peered at his screen and wrote down the details before giving the piece of paper to her with a shaking hand.

'Thank you.' Kay tucked the page into her notebook, then raised her chin. 'One final thing, Mr McDowell. Where were you between the hours of three o'clock and seven o'clock yesterday morning?'

McDowell swallowed. 'I was at home asleep until the alarm went off at five, then I came in here and worked out until it was time to open at six-thirty.'

'Can anyone vouch for you?'

'My wife will, and we've got CCTV cameras all around the building – you'll see me on those.'

'Thank you, Mr McDowell.' Kay snapped shut her notebook. 'That will be all.'

CHAPTER FIVE

Kay hurried across Jubilee Square, then slowed as she approached Gabriel's Hill, wary of the cobblestones under her low heels and determined not to wrench her ankle.

It'd be sheer bad luck if she injured herself before the charity run and after last night's training session left her with sore calves, she was determined to up the ante on her regime.

Leaving the incident room to buy a cheap sandwich, she had paused on the way back at a favourite franchise and purchased coffee for herself and Higgins, grateful that the police constable had offered to make phone calls to the people on Dean McDowell's list of runners while she had fought her way through another list generated by calls to the Crimestoppers number set up for the enquiry.

They were winning the relentless battle with

information by the time Sharp had commented on her stomach rumbling and told her to take a break – and the takeout coffee was better than the stuff in the vending machine outside the incident room.

Kay huffed her fringe out of her eyes and bit back a sense of frustration at the lack of progress.

Her mobile phone began to vibrate in her bag, and she paused to switch both takeout cups to one hand before rummaging in the side pocket and pressing the answer button before it went to voicemail.

'Hunter.'

'Only me.'

She recognised Higgins' voice and moved to the side of the pavement out of the way of an oncoming gaggle of teenagers in school uniforms. 'I'll be back in a sec. I'm nearly there.'

'I guessed that, but I've been told to head over to Headquarters – they need cover over there for the rest of the shift.'

Kay eyed the hot drinks in her hand. 'Who gets your coffee?'

Higgins chuckled. 'Best give it to Sharp. Might keep you in his good books.'

'Very funny. Okay, what d'you need?'

'Just thought I'd give you an update before I disappear. I've finished speaking with the members of McDowell's gym who Dean said had signed up for the charity run – only one of them knew Laura by sight but confirms he never ran with her. He and his wife live out

Coxheath way and tend to train together or run with the local harriers' group every now and again. None of the others knew her or Sarah Anderson, and I've got alibis for all of them too. They all check out.'

Kay sighed. 'Okay. Worth a shot, anyway.'

'Hopefully, I'll be back in the morning – got to go.'

'Thanks.'

She ended the call, dropped her phone back in her bag and picked up her pace as her thoughts tumbled over each other.

Making a mental note to check that one of her colleagues had spoken to Laura's neighbours about her running habits and whether she had been seen leaving her house yesterday morning with anyone, Kay zig-zagged between the stationary traffic on Palace Avenue and sidled through the security gates to the police station as they opened to let a liveried patrol car out.

It paused next to her, the window lowering before an arm snaked out.

'I'll take it with me.'

She leaned in and handed over the coffee to Higgins. 'Sharp will be gutted he's missing out.'

'Don't tell him.'

Kay laughed as he pulled away, then frowned as she saw two figures emerge from a silver four-door vehicle at the far end of the car park.

Amber grinned at Kay as she drew closer. 'Hi, Hunter! How's your training going?'

'Okay, I suppose,' Kay said, then took a sip of coffee.

'Oh, I wouldn't drink that stuff if I were you.'

Amber wrinkled her nose. 'You'll dehydrate too fast – you need to stick to non-caffeinated herbal tea at the moment. That's what my personal trainer advises, anyway.'

'I'll bear that in mind, thanks.'

Hugh peered over his shoulder at the sound of her voice as he lifted a briefcase from the back seat, and Kay raised her chin so she could look him in the eye.

'I'd listen to her if I were you,' he said. 'Amber's hoping for a decent race against you on Saturday.'

Despite her natural competitiveness, Kay paused beside the lithe assistant forensic technician. 'You are taking all this seriously, aren't you, Amber? Making sure you don't run on your own, that sort of thing while we try to catch this bastard, I mean.'

The forensic assistant laughed. 'Oh, don't worry about me. I always make sure I run in a pair, anyway – it makes for a better training regime because I've got someone to pace with. You should try it sometime,' she added before turning on her heel and making her way over to the entrance to the police station.

Hugh swung shut the car door, aiming the key fob at the vehicle before grimacing at Kay.

'I really don't fancy your chances against her, Hunter.'

'Thanks a lot, Hugh.'

'Well, just so you know – there's a sweepstake going around the office.' He shrugged. 'Her odds are better than yours.'

Kay's mouth dropped open as he hurried after his colleague.

'Bloody great,' she muttered, then glanced at her watch and swore.

The briefing was due to start in five minutes.

CHAPTER SIX

Kay leaned her head against the bus window and watched the darkening Tonbridge skyline come into view, cursing the broken clutch that meant her car was in for repair, leaving her to rely on public transport that day.

The journey home took thirty-five minutes by train, but due to signalling works she was corralled onto a bus replacement service at Maidstone.

She swayed on her feet for the first few miles, hanging on to the back of a seat and jostling for elbow space with a crowd of disgruntled commuters, turning her face away from a large man with body odour as he'd leered at her.

Sinking into a spare seat at Wateringbury as soon as a woman rose to leave, Kay plucked the free newspaper she left behind and began flicking through the pages.

Most of it was regurgitated celebrity gossip, interspersed with a little news and advertisements for local businesses.

Her gaze wandered over the bright coloured boxes extolling the cost benefits of having her legs waxed ('A Massive 20% Off!') alongside the option of visiting a psychologist if Kay was over-stressed or trying to quit smoking (Kay wasn't, on both counts) until she turned the page, and stopped.

Kay swallowed and re-read the brightly-coloured print.

A split second later, her heart jumped.

Underneath a feature about the upcoming charity run, an advertisement had been placed. Surrounded by a bright red border, the wording leapt from the page, taunting her.

Get the best from your training. Download our free app. Map your route. Compare your times. Race your friends!

Below the wording, the advertisement reference had been displayed, together with a website address. No phone number.

Kay checked over her shoulder. The bus was empty now, save for a teenager listening to music at the far end, a faint *hiss-hiss* audible from where she sat.

She pulled out her phone, flicked to the front of the newspaper, and dialled the advertising manager's number, crossing her fingers that he'd be working late.

He was.

Kay identified herself, explained what she needed, and told him she'd be at his office with the relevant paperwork in the morning.

Her shift was three hours old by the time she'd found Higgins, explained he was coming with her for the day, assuring him she meant work, nothing else, and made her way across town to meet with the advertising manager of the free newspaper.

Chatting with the newspaper executive resulted in them being given the name and address of the man who had placed the advertisement and after she'd explained her theory to Sharp, he'd sent them away to investigate further.

Fifty-five minutes later, Higgins swung the car into a leafy cul-de-sac, slowed at the kerb, and turned off the engine.

They sat for a moment, eyeing up the properties on the small street.

The front gardens varied from being lovingly tended to the unfenced basics of the house in front of them.o

'Background check confirms Cameron Ashe and his

wife have been renting here for three months,' said Higgins, his hands still on the steering wheel as he peered up at the bedroom windows. 'No kids. Moved down from Bolton.'

'Any pets?'

'No, so we don't have to worry about dogs attacking us.'

'Just as well. Right, let's do this,' Kay said, opening her door. 'And if you think of anything I need to ask about this app of his and I don't raise it, feel free to chime in.'

'Will do.'

After Higgins rang the doorbell, they stood on the front step for a couple of minutes before the door swung open, and a thin man of medium height peered out at them through bloodshot eyes.

His hair awry, he frowned, tucked his stained T-shirt into his jeans, the pushed his glasses back up his nose.

'Can I help you?'

Kay introduced Higgins and herself before she held up the newspaper clipping. 'Mr Ashe – can you please confirm you placed this advertisement?'

He squinted, reached out and pulled her hand closer, then nodded. 'Yes, I did. What's this about?'

Kay lowered the newspaper. 'Could we come in, sir?'

'Sure, sure.'

He turned and led the way into a sparsely furnished living area, the paintwork beige and the carpet threadbare. Within six paces, he'd reached the kitchen worktops and turned back to them.

'Did you want tea or anything?'

'No, thanks – that won't be necessary,' Kay said. 'We'd like to ask you some questions about your running app.'

He nodded. 'Okay. Why don't you come through to the office, then?'

With that, he opened the back door and walked outside.

Kay turned to Higgins, raised an eyebrow, and then followed Ashe.

They traipsed across an overgrown garden until they caught up with him outside a cinderblock shed.

He turned to them, his hand on the door handle. 'The last place we rented had an office in the house. Best we could afford down here was this. It's warm and dry, though.'

He flicked on a switch as he led the way into the small space, and a fluorescent strip light blinked into life above their heads. He waved them onto two packing cases next to his desk, while he sat on a battered office chair.

The desk was a simple set-up – computer and screen, three drawers under the desk, and a filing tray rack next to the computer hard drive.

Ashe rubbed his hands on his thighs as they lowered themselves into their makeshift seats, and Kay nodded to Higgins as he pulled out his notebook and pen.

After Ashe had given them the potted history of how he'd left school, joined an IT company, then left that to pursue a career writing apps for smartphones a year ago,

Kay brought his attention back to the newspaper advertisement.

'So, this running app,' Kay said. 'From what I understand, it records people's routes, and they can keep track of their times and see how they're improving, right?'

'Yes.'

'Do you pass on that information to any third parties?'

'No, that's not allowed,' he said. 'There are strict data protection laws against doing that.'

'But you do collect the data?'

'Yes.'

'Can you show me?'

'Of course. Hang on.'

He spun around on his chair, then wiggled the mouse on the desk until the computer burst to life.

Kay watched, his movements swift and precise as he brought up the programme on the screen. She stood, moving closer until she was standing at his shoulder and could see what he was doing.

'This is the background part of the app programme,' he explained. 'All the users' information is stored here.'

'What sort of data do you collect?'

'Names, addresses – not credit card details, those are held by third party payment servers for security purposes,' he explained. 'And then we keep records of their routes, including their favourite ones, personal best times, and any other training data they want to record.'

'Why collect so much information if you don't intend to pass it on to third parties?' asked Higgins.

Kay held up her thumb to him behind Ashe's back, lowering her hand as the IT expert turned.

'In case users lose their running data,' he said. 'We provide a full back-up service with the app, so if users lose their phone or change it, we can transfer the data over for them.'

'Is it possible, then, for you to monitor, say, one particular runner's progress over time?' Kay asked. 'Just by analysing the historical data the app records?'

'Yes. We don't use it, but the coding programme is set up to be able to do that.'

Kay's head jerked up at the sound of a gate being slammed shut and footsteps in the yard outside.

'Ah, that'll be my wife, Cheryl,' said Ashe, standing.

Kay glanced at Higgins, and then watched as Ashe moved to the door.

'I'm in here, love.'

A petite redhead appeared in the doorway, her long hair tied back in a ponytail, her arms and legs muscular and tanned poking out from designer-labelled running shorts and a T-shirt.

Kay sensed her own calf muscles grow flabbier as she looked at her.

There was nothing like meeting a serious athlete when you were several weeks behind on your own training regime.

'Cheryl does all the book-keeping for the business,' Ashe explained after introducing them.

'I work part-time a couple of days a week and then look after Cameron's business the rest of the time in between training,' Cheryl added, flicking her hair over her shoulder and brushing her palm over her forehead to slick away imaginary sweat.

'And you did this in Bolton as well?'

He nodded. 'Yes. Cheryl missed the warmer weather down here, though, so we decided to move back a few months ago.' His nose wrinkled as he glanced around at the meagre office space. 'Hopefully, the business will grow, and we can afford a place of our own soon.'

Kay nodded to Higgins. 'I think we're done here, Constable Higgins.' Kay turned to Ashe and his wife. 'Thank you for your time, Mr Ashe. Can you confirm the telephone number we can reach you on if we have further questions?'

'Sure.' He moved past her, leaned across the desk, and scribbled on a notepad before tearing out the page and handing it to her.

'Thank you.' Kay turned to Cheryl. 'Do you use your husband's app for your training?'

She laughed. 'Oh no – I don't understand smartphones at all,' she said. 'I've still got one of those old flip-open ones. It makes phone calls and sends texts. That's it.'

'Cheryl's a great book-keeper, but all the technology stuff goes over her head, doesn't it, love?' Ashe smiled, putting his arm around his wife's waist.

She smiled at him before turning her attention back to Kay.

'He's right, it does. I haven't got a clue.'

CHAPTER EIGHT

'Do you know what I think? I reckon that after he's got all the information from the app, he can analyse it to find out where women are running, what times they run at, and how fast they run.'

Kay finished talking and waited while Sharp scribbled on the whiteboard, re-capped the pen, and picked up his coffee.

'So, routine is their killer, is that what you're saying?' asked Higgins.

Kay turned in her seat to face her colleague and leaned an arm over the back. 'Exactly, and he's using the app to track their movements. I know what I'm like when I'm out for a run – I have favourite routes, especially since I've been training for the charity race.'

'Then we know how to draw him out, don't we, Hunter?'

Kay turned at the sound of Sharp's voice. Her eyes widened as her thought processes caught up.

'Really?' Her eyes narrowed. 'How?'

'I executed a search warrant based on your report, and we've used that to request a copy of Ashe's database. We know all the routes his users take. All we need now is someone capable of running those routes.'

'You can't be serious.'

He folded his arms across his chest. 'I'm very serious,' he said, his smile disappearing. 'I think you've made a valid case for your theory. And we're out of time.' He pointed to the calendar on the wall. 'The charity run is on Saturday. If we don't catch him before then, based on your theory, we might lose him for good – because he'll move on. There isn't another race scheduled in this area until June.'

Her shoulders slumped.

'Kay.' Sharp crossed the space between them. He reached out and patted her shoulder, then pointed at the whiteboard. 'We'll be there with you. Based on what evidence we've got, we now know the sort of person he targets, and we can work out where the grab points are in each park.'

'We'll need to contact the women on that database,' Kay said. 'Advise them to stay away from their usual routes and stop using the app until we've got him in custody.'

'Higgins can do that while we're setting up the operation,' said Sharp, clicking his fingers at the young constable.

Kay sighed. She knew he was right. 'I just feel uncomfortable being used as bait.'

A frown creased Sharp's brow before he spoke. 'At least you know what you're getting into,' he said. 'Those two women didn't.'

Kay closed her eyes, ashamed. 'Yes, Sarge.'

He moved away, gathered up the files on his desk and turned towards the door. 'I'll bring the DI up to speed on our proposal.' He opened the door and paused. 'Good work, detective.'

Kay managed a small smile before he stalked from the room.

CHAPTER NINE

Her legs ached, her thighs burned, and Kay knew her face was beetroot red because even the sweat running down it was warm.

'Just another lap to go.' Sharp's voice fizzled through her earpiece.

Kay could hear laughter in the background and cursed them all while her shoes pounded the concrete bike path.

The sun had disappeared over the horizon an hour ago, and as soon as Sharp had received confirmation from the Kent Police digital forensic experts that they'd hacked the app and set up a new account for her, including a month-long running history, they set out to catch their killer.

In her other ear, the running app counted off the distance, a calm and collected female voice belonging to someone who, in Kay's opinion, had never run in her life.

'Okay, you're hitting the last two hundred metres,' said Sharp. 'Slow to a walk, and look exhausted.'

Kay choked out a response, slowed as he suggested, and walked until she found a bench she could stretch against.

A street lamp cast a pyramid of light around her, confining the surrounding parkland to darkness.

She forced down the panic that threatened to have her running in the opposite direction within seconds.

Instead, starting with her aching calf muscles, Kay began to stretch. She worked her way up until she was flexing her arms across her chest, and had just raised her hands above her head when the hairs on the back of her neck stood on end.

She cried out as Ashe emerged from the bushes behind the wooden seat, his hands in the pockets of his dark coloured jacket.

'Detective Hunter,' he said, ambling closer. 'I was hoping I'd see you here.'

Kay swallowed, Sharp's voice in her earpiece shouting, mobilising the team towards her position.

'Mr Ashe,' Kay spluttered. She coughed a couple of times to clear her throat and tried again. 'Hello – what are you doing here?'

'Don't run away.'

'What do you mean?'

He came closer. 'It's all right,' he said. 'I only wanted to talk to you.'

Kay narrowed her eyes. 'I gave you my business card.

You could have called me at the station or left a message for me.'

'It's much better if we talk here. Away from prying eyes.'

'I really don't think that's a good idea,' Kay said, backing away.

He held up his hand. 'No – really, I just want to talk.'

He drew closer, a desperate look in his eyes, and a small smile etched across his lips.

Kay caught movement in her peripheral vision and jerked her arm away, Ashe's fingers brushing against her skin.

'Please – we need to talk,' he urged.

'Don't touch me,' Kay hissed, backing away.

'It's okay. I won't hurt you,' he said. 'Shall we sit down?'

'No.'

'Please,' he said. 'It'll only take a minute, I promise.'

She fought down the urge to put into practice the self-defence training she'd received at the refresher course only two months ago, instead of giving him the impression she was weak. She took a step backwards.

Ashe lurched towards her with both arms open wide.

'No! Leave me alone!'

Her cries were cut short by a series of shouts – voices from the dark parkland behind her and further along the bike path.

Kay moved fast, blocking Ashe's escape back into the bushes, trying to make her slight frame intimidating.

Ashe spun round to face her, his face stricken. 'Don't do this – you're making a terrible mistake!'

'I don't think so,' Kay gasped as a dark shape pushed past her.

Higgins launched his body at Ashe, pulling the man to the ground, sending both of them tumbling into the long grass behind the bench.

As Higgins pulled the software engineer to his feet, Sharp slid to a stop next to her.

'Are you okay?'

Kay nodded. 'I think so, Sarge. He scared me.'

'You did good,' said Sharp. 'Let's go back to the station and see what he has to say for himself.'

CHAPTER TEN

When Kay walked through the door into the observation room, she saw that DC Richard Christie had joined Sharp in interview room two, his pen hovering over his notepad.

On screen, at the table opposite two detectives and with a duty solicitor beside him, Ashe groaned and held his head in his hands, keeping his gaze lowered.

Kay put down her coffee cup, leaned forward and turned up the volume.

'Interview commences at eight forty-two,' said Sharp, pushing the record button on the machine next to him, and then indicating to the detective constable beside him to begin.

'First of all, Mr Ashe, we'd like to know why you were following our colleague in the park tonight?' Christie narrowed his eyes. 'Why did you approach her?'

Heat rose to the other man's face under the detectives' scrutiny. 'I-I was testing a new update to the app, that's all. I happened to see her, and I wondered if perhaps I might be able to help with your investigation.'

'In what way?'

'Well, I thought if we told female runners in the area that the new update enables them to share their route with their friends in real-time, rather than retrospectively like the old version, it'd help them.' Ashe looked from Christie to Sharp. 'It's a safety feature, you see? They wouldn't feel like they were running alone.'

'Hardly appropriate to accost one of our officers at night with a marketing spiel,' said Sharp.

'So, Mr Ashe,' said Christie. 'How long have you been tracking your victims using your software?'

'I haven't, I swear.'

'Is this why you had to move from Bolton two months ago?'

Sharp leaned across the desk. 'Tell us, Ashe,' he said. 'If we phone our colleagues up in Lancashire, are we going to hear a similar story to our two murders?'

Ashe sighed and raised his head. 'It's not what you think.'

Christie turned at a knock at the door, his concentration broken.

Higgins appeared. 'Apologies for interrupting, Sarge, but could I have a word?'

'Interview paused at eight-fifty,' said Sharp, hitting the stop button.

Christie followed him through the door and closed it behind him.

Kay shot from her seat, reaching the corridor outside at the same time as the two detectives.

'What is it?'

Higgins glanced from her to Sharp, and then back, before drawing a long breath.

'There's been another murder,' he said. 'In a park two miles from where we picked up Mr Ashe.'

Kay blinked, the corridor lights suddenly too bright. 'When?'

'The body was discovered by a dog walker twenty minutes ago,' said Higgins. 'The call's only just been routed through to us from Headquarters.'

Sharp's shoulders sagged.

'All right, Christie,' he said. 'Let's get back in there and tell Mr Ashe he'll be staying with us for a while yet. Then we'll go to the scene.'

'Shall I drive, Sarge?' said Kay.

The detective sergeant paused with his hand on the door to the interview room, then glanced over his shoulder. 'No need, Kay. Get yourself home. It's been a long day.'

Kay bit her lip as the door closed behind the two men, and rubbed her arms before walking back to the incident room, her stomach churning.

Another woman dead, and it was all her fault.

CHAPTER ELEVEN

Kay aimed the remote controller at the television and jabbed at the buttons.

Her running shoes sat next to the front door and from the kitchen, she could hear the washing machine on its final spin as the theme tune to a murder mystery series began to ring out.

She sighed at the screen, switched the channel and threw the remote onto a small wooden table next to her feet before picking up the large glass of red she'd poured ten minutes ago.

A half-eaten Chinese takeaway sat next to her mobile phone, the prawn dish growing cold as her appetite waned.

No-one had said anything to her when she collected her bag and coat from the incident room, but she could sense them all looking at her.

Sharp had passed her at the bottom of the stairs, ignoring her as he raised his mobile phone to his ear. It was DC Christie who told her Cameron Ashe had been released, pending further enquiries.

Face reddening, Kay had scuttled out of the back door of the police station and up the hill to the bus stop, sure that her fellow travellers could sense her embarrassment.

She eyed the leftover takeaway and wondered if it would keep until the next night.

Chances were, she was in for some more late shifts.

Her mobile phone vibrated on the table, and she groaned at the name displayed on the screen before answering.

'Hello, Mum.'

'You sound tired.'

It was an accusation, not an observation. Her mother's voice held no warmth, no concern, and Kay winced at the harsh pitch.

'I'm fine. Long day, that's all.'

'I knew you weren't cut out for this sort of thing,' her mother scolded. 'It's not too late to do something else with your life, you know. You're only twenty-seven.'

'Did you want something?'

'Can't I call to see how you are?'

'I'm okay.'

'Not by the sound of it. Why don't you find a nice job? Something nine to five that will give you a chance to have a bit of a social life? You haven't had a boyfriend in ages, have you?'

'How's Dad?' she managed.

'Down the pub playing darts. I don't know why – he

needs to lose weight. I keep telling him it's not healthy to go down there all the time. He says it's to give me some peace and quiet...'

Kay rolled her eyes. 'Mum, I've got to go. Busy day tomorrow, and I'm due in early.'

'That's what I'm saying, Kay. Find something else to do. Something you're good at...'

Kay ended the call while her mother was in the middle of saying her goodbyes and tossed aside the phone.

'Bloody hell,' she mumbled and wiped tears of frustration from her cheeks.

Three months since her training had ended, and she could feel her initial confidence and excitement ebbing away.

She had been so sure that Ashe was their suspect, so sure that his app was the link between the murders, that she had made a catastrophic mistake and caused another woman's death.

She sniffed, then picked up her wineglass and padded through to the kitchen, topping it up with the last of the Shiraz before re-capping the bottle.

She set it down with a clatter on the worktop and blinked.

What if the murders weren't connected?

How on earth were they going to catch a killer who murdered at random?

The next morning, Kay swiped her security card over the panel beside the reception desk and held open the door for a pair of uniformed constables, their arms laden with cardboard boxes.

They raced up the stairs leading to the incident rooms, their boots thumping across the thin carpet when they reached the floor above.

'What's all that about?' she said.

'A raid over at Paddock Wood. Money laundering or something,' said Sergeant Maurice Hoyle. He turned away from the reception desk and rested his arm on the counter. 'Are you all right? You had a face like thunder when you left here last night.'

'Bad day.'

'Ah. I heard a suspect was released last night – was he one of yours?'

'I thought he was our killer.'

The older sergeant's face softened. 'And then someone else died, right?'

She nodded.

'I hope someone told you it wasn't your fault,' he said.

'That doesn't make it any better.'

'No, but it does give you a reason to get upstairs and get back to work, doesn't it? They're not going to catch the real killer without you. All hands on deck, and all that.'

Kay forced a smile and patted her fist against the door frame. 'Speaking of which, I should get going.'

'Before you do, I overheard Higgins saying that you were worrying about your training for the charity run with everything else going on.'

'Just a bit.' She sighed. 'I said to him yesterday that I went out for a run on my own the other night, and there was hardly anyone else around. I don't see myself using that app any time soon, either.'

'You should do what my wife does – she belongs to a running group on social media. They arrange to go out in pairs, especially at the moment. If they do prefer to run alone then they post their route and what time they expect to be back so if they don't check in on their return, someone can raise the alarm for them.' He smiled. 'Of course, it's not all serious – they post their progress as well, best times, things like that. Sophie enjoys it because it keeps her motivated, and it keeps me happy because someone always knows where she is.'

He reached out for a piece of paper and scrawled

across it. 'This is the group. All you do is send them a request to join and someone will approve it. I'll tell Sophie to keep a look out for you if you like.'

'Thanks, Maurice – appreciate it. I'll take a look later.'

Kay hurried up the stairs and into the incident room, switching on her computer while she shrugged her arms out of her coat before hanging it over the back of her chair.

A general hubbub of noise filled the space, and despite the paranoia seeping through her thoughts none of her colleagues had seized upon the chance to tease her about her error the night before.

Instead, grim faces peered at computer screens while phones rang, and urgent conversations swept over her as she worked her way through her emails and the tasks that were delegated to her through the Home Office Large Major Enquiry System.

It was going to be a busy day.

CHAPTER THIRTEEN

'I got you cheese and tomato – that all right?'

Kay looked up from her computer screen at the sound of DC Christie's voice, and stifled a yawn.

'Brilliant, thanks, Rich.'

He handed her the wrapped sandwich then pulled across a spare chair, the casters rattling over a protective rubber mat placed under the desk by the previous occupant.

'How're you doing?'

'All right,' she said between mouthfuls. She swallowed, then pointed at the screen. 'I've cross-referenced the gyms again, but our third victim – Alicia Martin – hadn't been to the gym she belonged to in over four months.'

'Any idea why?'

'The owner there said it's common – people join up in the New Year and get all excited about a new routine before they start to drift away. He reckons memberships like that cover his overheads for six months.'

Christie grimaced. 'I think the bloke who owns my local gym would say the same thing.'

Kay reached into her tray and pulled out a folder full of witness statements. 'I've been reading through the statements uniform took last night, too. None of the property owners along that stretch of footpath heard anything or saw anything suspicious. If it wasn't for that dog-walker...'

'Alicia might've lain there all night before she was discovered.' Christie pushed his chair back and rose, straightening his jacket. 'Good work, anyway.'

'Rich?' Kay scrunched up the empty sandwich wrapper in her hand and took a deep breath. 'I'm sorry about yesterday. I screwed up.'

'No, you didn't. It was a valid lead, and it needed to be actioned. You did the right thing in the circumstances. Ashe wasn't exactly acting rationally by approaching you in the park, either, so...'

'But Alicia––'

'Would've died anyway. We had nothing to suggest she was going to be the next victim – or any other suspects.' He gave the chair a shove, sending it to a shuddering standstill under the neighbouring desk. 'What would you have done in Sharp's shoes if someone had come to you with the same information?'

Kay exhaled. 'Acted on it.'

'There you go, then.' He winked. 'Don't stay too late

tonight. We need you bright-eyed and bushy-tailed back here in the morning.'

Despite Christie's advice, the incident room was almost deserted by the time Kay looked at the time on her computer screen and realised it was seven o'clock.

Beyond the windows, a light fog smudged the orange glow from sodium streetlights and somewhere within the building, a vacuum cleaner hummed as the cleaners worked.

'Night, Kay.' Higgins held up his hand as he walked towards the door, a black backpack slung over one shoulder.

'Night.'

She scrolled the mouse over the screen, closing different apps and windows, and wondered whether to find somewhere to have dinner in town before heading home or order a takeaway.

She groaned. A takeaway two nights in a row, and her race on Saturday would suffer.

Unless she went for a run before heading home – she

kept a spare pair of trainers and clothes in her locker downstairs.

Decision made, she reached out to turn off her computer and then froze.

The piece of paper Maurice handed to her that morning was tucked under her desk phone, the name of the social media group stark under the harsh office lighting.

Kay glanced over her shoulder.

The incident room was empty now, Higgins being the only one who had stayed behind so he could enter the last of the phone enquiries received that afternoon into the HOLMES2 database.

Her eyes fell on the calendar next to her computer screen.

The charity run was only three days away, and Alicia's murder had taken place within three days of Laura's.

There had been a week between Laura's murder and the first.

Were the murders getting closer together because the race date was drawing near?

Was someone else going to die tonight?

Heart racing, she hurried over to the whiteboard at the far end of the room, swearing under her breath as her leg struck the corner of a colleague's desk in her haste to reach it.

Rubbing her thigh, she ran her eyes over the map, the pins denoting where the victims were found, and the red marker pen lines that Sharp had added to highlight the area where the killer appeared to be operating.

It was a few miles in diameter, but it would do.

Kay returned to her desk, threw herself into her chair and pulled her keyboard towards her.

She clicked on the internet browser on her screen, logged in to the social media site, and searched for running groups in the town.

Maurice's wife's group was one of the top results, but Kay avoided that.

She needed to find one whose members ran in the same area where the three victims were found, and she needed to act fast.

Kay scrolled through the list of four groups, clicking on each and then discarding the link when she found the group's members lived outside of the killer's circle.

She found the group she sought on her fifth attempt and sent a request to join.

It didn't take long.

A notification appeared in the top left of the screen within seconds.

Kay took a deep breath, then picked up her mobile phone and found Sharp's number.

It went straight to voicemail.

'Dammit.'

She tapped the phone against her chin for a moment, then dialled DC Christie's number.

Engaged.

Kay drummed her fingers on the desk.

Of course, they could be talking to each other –

catching up before the morning's briefing. Or both of them could be talking to someone else.

She closed her eyes for a moment, then opened them and squared her shoulders.

This couldn't wait.

She clicked on a space on the social media group's main page to add a new post and introduced herself as someone new to the area – easy enough to do, as she was rarely on the site and her personal profile was set to private.

Going out for a run tonight – been too scared to lately but if I don't, I won't be ready for Saturday's race, she began.

She added the route she planned to take, then sat back and read through the words.

A predatory smile twitched at her lips.

I reckon if I train tonight and rest tomorrow, I'll easily be in the top three to finish – maybe I'll even win! she typed, and for good measure added a grinning emoji.

'That should work, you bastard.'

CHAPTER FIFTEEN

Kay rested her foot on a concrete bollard blocking vehicle access into the park and re-laced her shoes.

It gave her a chance to scan her surroundings, although the thickening fog meant she could only see a hundred metres in each direction.

The car park was deserted save for her own vehicle, a new clutch fitted and her bank account five hundred pounds lighter.

In the distance, she heard a solitary truck engine as its driver changed gear to counteract the steep climb up the hill past the park, the sound muffled by the fog.

Her breath misted as she took a gulp of air, exhaling to try to release some of the stress clutching at her limbs as she took in the muted outlines of trees lining the footpath, ghostly silhouettes against the streetlights overhead that struggled to pierce the gloom.

'Okay, Hunter,' she muttered, zipping up her car

keys and mobile phone within her sweatshirt pockets. 'Enough stalling.'

She set herself an easy pace to begin with, the route clear in her mind.

The footpath made for smooth progress and when she glanced over her shoulder she was shocked to find she could no longer see her car.

Ahead, the path curved around to the left and away from the back gardens that bordered the park.

For the next half a mile, she would be alone.

She increased her stride, her leg muscles warming up and easing into the familiar training routine.

Any other time, she knew she would enjoy the chance to discover a new route but paranoia was already beginning to set in.

Should she have waited and tried again to phone Sharp and Christie?

Should she have posted the challenge to the killer in the first place?

She slowed to a walk, then stopped as the realisation hit her that she had no idea what she was going to do when or if she did confront the killer.

'Kay.'

She froze, peering into the gloom, her heart pounding. 'Who's there?'

A figure loomed out from the fog, moving closer from behind the abandoned swing set to her left and advancing towards her.

Kay took a step back, her mouth falling open at the sight of the familiar face.

'Amber? What're you doing here?'

CHAPTER SIXTEEN

‘More to the point, Hunter – why are you here?’

The trainee crime scene technician stepped closer, then shrugged open her waterproof running jacket and pulled out a baseball bat.

Kay’s eyes widened, and she held up her hands. ‘I fancied a run after work, that’s all. You?’

‘You’re a liar, Hunter.’ Amber flicked her long blonde hair over her shoulder. ‘Thought you’d try to catch a killer on your own, did you?’

Kay moved to the side and looked left and right but there was no-one else there.

No-one to save her.

She cursed at her own stupidity.

If she tried to scream, no-one would hear her.

The thick fog would deafen the sound, mask her cries for help.

‘I can explain, Amber.’

‘Go on, then.’

'I just wanted to try to stop anyone else getting hurt. I thought if I could––'

'Set a trap? Catch a killer on your own?' Amber cocked her head to one side. 'Did you really think you were that good?'

'How did you know I'd be here?'

'That's *my* running group,' the woman hissed. 'Mine.'

Kay let out a shaking laugh. 'My God, that's it, isn't it? That's how you've been picking out your victims. Anyone who posts a better time than you, and you kill them.' She frowned. 'Why?'

'Because I can.' Amber swung the baseball bat against a rhododendron bush, sending leaves flying over the footpath. 'Because I like it. Because it stops anyone from beating me to the finish line.'

'You're sick,' said Kay, unable to keep the disgust from her voice.

Amber laughed and took another swipe at the plant.

'You need to get help,' said Kay. 'I can help you. We'll go to Sharp together...'

'No.' Amber spun around to face her, her eyes wild. 'You're not going anywhere.'

Kay took a step back and held up her hands, her mouth dry as she realised she'd miscalculated.

There would be no negotiation.

No making Amber see sense.

No way out.

The woman leapt forward, and Kay felt a dull ache against the side of her head as she turned to run.

She stumbled, scraping her hands on the stony ground as she fell, crying out as her ankle twisted.

'You had to be better, didn't you?' Amber sneered, swinging the baseball bat from side to side. 'You couldn't help yourself, rubbing it in everyone's face that you were going to do so well this weekend, and poking around instead of minding your own business.'

Kay shuffled backwards, her elbows digging into the soft turf while her ankles tried to find purchase.

A darkness flashed across Amber's face then and she snarled, raising the baseball bat above her head.

'I'm better than you,' she spat. 'And now I always will be.'

Kay screamed and raised her arm as the bat swung down, then gasped as a shadow shot out from the fog and tackled Amber to the ground.

The baseball bat clattered to the footpath.

Kay pushed herself to her feet and bit back a cry as a jolt of pain shot through her leg.

Amber was shrieking as she punched and kicked at her assailant – but he was too strong for her.

He flipped her onto her stomach, then pinned her down with his knees and peered over his shoulder to where Kay stood, her mouth open in surprise.

'Hunter, for chrissakes,' he gasped. 'Handcuffs – back pocket.'

'Sarge?'

CHAPTER SEVENTEEN

Kay winced as Higgins patted a cotton wool ball soaked in antiseptic lotion against the cuts on her face, then held up her hand to stop him as a familiar figure appeared at the open door to the observation room.

Hugh Hughes had aged since she'd last seen him, the crime scene investigator's face a sickly grey as he eyed the bruises forming on her arms.

'Kay, I'm so sorry – I had no idea. I––'

'None of us did, Hugh. It's okay.'

His shoulders slumped. 'Even so. There'll be an enquiry.'

'You weren't to blame for any of this. Have you spoken with Sharp?'

'Yes – he's just finished taking my formal statement. I'm about to head home, and then I expect I'll be asked to attend a professional hearing at some point.'

'She fooled us all, didn't she?'

'None more so than me, Kay. Sharp thinks she got a

kick out of carrying out her victims' own crime scene investigations and trying to outsmart us.' He shivered. 'She's been working here for eight months. God knows how many more she's killed.'

'She'll be put away for a long time,' said Kay. 'We'll make sure of that.'

He gave her a sad smile. 'Look after yourself.'

Higgins turned to her as the pathologist left, his eyes wide. 'Bloody hell. Can't imagine what he's going through at the moment.'

'I know.' Kay yelped as he applied more antiseptic to a scratch above her eyebrow. 'And stop that – you're enjoying it too much.'

CHAPTER EIGHTEEN

'Kay?'

She turned at the sound of Sharp's voice to see him hurrying down the stairs towards her.

'Sarge?'

He led her away from the front desk. 'Let's talk outside.'

Kay frowned, but fell into step beside him.

'Amber has confessed to the three murders,' he said. 'We found the victims' mobile phones in her locker. She deleted the posts they wrote in her social media group after she targeted them.'

Kay swallowed. 'Jesus, Sarge.'

He said nothing further as they headed out of the front door.

When they reached the kerb, he waited until two uniformed constables had passed, then turned to her.

'Don't ever take a risk like that again, Kay.'

'I tried to phone you, Sarge. And Richard. Both of your phones were engaged.'

'You should've waited.'

'I'm sorry, Sarge, but I was worried if I did, we'd miss the opportunity and she'd kill again.'

'She very nearly did. If it wasn't for the fact my wife Rebecca follows the same social media group that you posted in and told me what you wrote in there––'

Kay blinked, the realisation smacking her in the chest.

'I've taken the liberty of ordering a taxi for you,' Sharp said. 'It's late, I'm not letting you drive after that strike to your head, and I don't want you travelling on public transport, not after what you've been through tonight. I'll have someone fetch your car for you and bring it back here.'

'Okay, thanks.'

He nodded, then scuffed the toe of his shoe against the bottom step, his hands in his pockets.

Eventually, he spoke.

'Look, one day you'll be in my shoes,' said Sharp, 'and you'll be telling your team the same thing, believe me. Don't risk your life – or that of your colleagues. It might be one of us who has to deal with the aftermath.'

'I understand.'

He nodded, then turned as a taxi pulled up to the kerb. 'Here's your ride – and here's twenty quid towards the fare.'

'Sarge, you don't have to do that.'

Sharp grinned and held open the passenger door for her.

'Trust me, I do. At least that way, I know you'll get home safe.'

Kay smiled as she got in, then wound down the window.

'Thanks, Sarge. For everything. See you tomorrow.'

THE END

BLOOD ON SNOW

The car slewed to a begrudging standstill, the tyres sinking into fresh snow two inches thick and unspoilt.

Beyond the windscreen stood a modest three-bedroom suburban home with a white topping of flakes covering the roof tiles, icicle-shaped Christmas fairy lights dangling from the windowsills battling for space with the real thing.

The middle house was identical to four others in the small crescent-shaped street – except for the uniformed police officers and white-suited crime scene investigators crowding the driveway and postage stamp-sized front garden.

To the left of the vehicle, separating the crescent from the busy main road, was a grass-covered area housing a council rubbish bin and a bus shelter.

The grass had been churned up into a mixture of snow and mud – no doubt a snowball fight had been underway earlier that morning. A group of children held aloft mobile phones while they walked towards the secondary school farther along the road, their expressions bored rather than curious.

Probationary Detective Constable Kay Hunter paused with her hand on the car door handle and turned to her colleague, wool from her navy scarf sticking to her chapped lips before she brushed it out of the way.

'What do we know so far?'

Police Constable Simon Higgins tucked his radio into his stab vest and reached for his hat. 'The first responders got here half an hour ago. A woman, Liz Carter, was found dead in her back garden. The husband phoned 999 at ten past eight. They've got two teenagers – a boy of thirteen, and a fifteen-year-old daughter.'

'Bloody hell.' Kay heaved the door open, a blast of ice cold air filling the vehicle. 'Okay, let's go and find Sharp.'

Her foot slipped on the icy surface of the road as she got out, and she threw her hands out to the sides to regain her balance before falling into step beside Higgins.

She flashed her warrant card to the young PC guarding the taped-off concrete driveway, then signed the crime scene log he held out.

'Kay, we're through here.'

Detective Sergeant Devon Sharp waited at the front door, beckoning to her.

Ex-military police, ramrod straight with the first signs of grey at his temples, he stood to one side as she entered a bright hallway decorated with tinsel pinned in zigzag patterns across the ceiling.

Low voices mumbled through a door to her left,

while two abandoned backpacks lay next to the bottom tread of the staircase on her right.

'DC Christie's speaking to the husband and kids,' Sharp murmured. 'Come through to the kitchen and I'll show you what we've got so far.'

Kay kept her hands shoved in her pockets and followed him, her gaze roaming the family photographs hanging on the wall as she passed.

Liz Carter was a stylish brunette in her forties and in all the pictures had her arms draped around two kids who shared her toothy smile. Beside them, Andrew Carter towered above his wife, his close-cropped hair doing little to disguise a receding hairline.

Turning away at the sound of a polite cough, Kay edged sideways to let a CSI technician pass then blinked as she recognised the lanky form of Hugh Hughes.

'I didn't know you were at work this week,' she said.

'This morning,' Hugh replied, peering over his glasses at her as he pulled away his mask. 'Hell of a way to start the day.'

'Kay?'

She hurried to catch up with Sharp, entering a light and airy kitchen that appeared to have had a recent renovation.

A centre worktop ran the length of the room and led to patio doors, both of which were open.

She shivered, and followed her DS as he strode out into the garden and paused beside three stone steps bordered with snow-topped shrubs.

A second cordon of crime tape separated them from

a team of four CSIs who crouched a few yards from where Kay stood, their backs to her as they trod a demarcated path between the house and the woman's body.

'You missed Lucas,' said Sharp. 'He got another call out near Sheppey, but he reckons she died from a single blow to the head.'

Kay winced. 'Did she die straight away?'

'You know what these Home Office pathologists are like. He won't confirm it until after he's conducted the post mortem tomorrow morning but he thinks it was instant, yes.'

He moved to one side, and Kay swallowed.

Liz Carter lay on her back, her blank eyes staring up at the grey sky, a strand of hair across her forehead matted with viscous blood that had splattered the front of her shirt. Her arms were outstretched like a snow angel as if she had tried to break her fall, her mouth open in shock.

Kay wanted to wrap the woman in a soft blanket to shield her from the biting wind, noting she only wore slip-on patent shoes that matched her tailored suit trousers.

'Have they found a weapon?'

'Not yet.' Sharp peered over her shoulder. 'Here's Richard.'

Kay turned as DC Christie walked out of the kitchen and headed towards them, his face grim. 'The husband, Andrew, says he was in the shower when it happened. The two kids – Michael and Stephanie – were in the living room eating breakfast and watching television.

Andrew noticed the back doors were open when he came downstairs, and that's when he found his wife.'

'Did he have any idea what she was doing out here?' said Sharp.

'They adopted a cat last week. Apparently it kept getting out and she was afraid it'd go missing if it escaped.' Christie snapped shut his notebook. 'He thinks she went out after it to get it to come back inside before they went to work.'

Turning back to face the garden, Sharp let out a sigh. 'All right, you two. No sign of a weapon, and this garden isn't accessible via a gate. The only way in and out of here is through the house.'

'The kids say they had the living room door open while they were having breakfast,' said Christie. 'No-one came in through the front door – and Andrew confirms it was locked anyway. It always is until they leave to go to work and drop the kids off to school.'

'Jesse!'

A girl's voice shouted from inside the house a split second before a tabby-coloured blur shot past Kay's legs and onto the snow-covered lawn.

'Christ, there goes the crime scene,' said Sharp as the four CSIs rose to their feet and tried to usher the cat away from the taped-off area.

Kay spun around at the sound of footsteps and closed the patio doors as a teenaged girl slid to a halt on the tiled floor.

Shaking her head, holding out her arms to try to block the view of the garden, Kay waited until Andrew

Carter guided his daughter away, and bit back a sigh of relief.

'Did she see?' Sharp's voice held a note of panic.

'I don't think so.' Kay straightened her coat and walked over to where the DS and Christie stood on the steps, their faces concerned. 'I think I got there in time.'

'Thank God for that.'

Kay sidled closer, peering past his shoulder to where one of the CSIs was wrestling with the cat in his arms, a fresh trail of paw prints covering the snowy ground.

She frowned. 'Sarge? No-one else has walked on that snow except the husband and the wife, right? Besides the cat, I mean.'

Sharp moved until he was standing next to her. 'That's right – the CSIs stuck to the demarcated path.'

'Then where are the killer's footprints?'

CHAPTER TWO

'Someone get that bloody camera crew away from here,' Sharp barked, his voice carrying over the uniformed officers milling about the front garden. 'And tell the Family Liaison Officer to close the living room curtains.'

He turned to Kay and Christie. 'Right, you two – split up and start talking to the neighbours. Kay, you take Higgins with you and speak to the owners of the house at the back of the Carters' home – the gardens border each other, so our killer may have escaped that way. Christie, you're with me – we'll start with next door, number four. Apparently the bloke at number two on the other side works night shifts and isn't home yet.'

'Okay, Sarge.' Kay wandered across the driveway to where Higgins hovered at the outer perimeter, and jerked her thumb over her shoulder. 'Simon, you're with me. Sharp wants us to interview the neighbours in the house behind this one.'

'Do you want to take the car?'

She took one look at the traffic streaming along the street beyond the crescent and the emergency vehicles clogging the kerb, and shook her head. 'It'll be quicker if we walk.'

Reaching the entrance to the crescent, she paused and extracted her notebook from her bag, then drew the cluster of five houses arching left to right, added the house numbers and put a pencil mark next to the Carters' house.

That done, she glanced up to see Higgins watching.

'Just getting my bearings,' she said.

'Does Sharp think the killer got away through one of the other gardens?'

'Maybe. Let's go.'

She kept up with the quick pace he set, taking care to avoid icy patches that were beginning to appear on the pavement as the snow melted under passing foot traffic.

They turned into a dead-end street that ran behind the crescent, the properties spaced farther apart than the neighbouring streets and with large gardens and driveways that swept out of sight behind brick walls or privet hedges. Here, the snow was thicker on the pavements, the tyre tracks in the road favouring the left-hand side as residents had negotiated the icy conditions to begin their morning commute.

'This is the one.' Kay paused outside a mock-Tudor home, a gravel path leading to the front door.

Edging past a modern-looking camper van parked outside the garage, she rang the bell beside a glass-panelled door and took a step back, eyeing the six-foot-high fencing that stretched from each side of the house, shielding the back garden from view.

A fuzzy shape emerged from behind the glass before the door swung open and a man in his sixties peered out at them, his expression confused.

'We're not interested in buying anything, whatever it is you're selling.'

Kay held up her warrant card. 'Mr––'

'Wayne Starling.'

'Detective Constable Kay Hunter, and this is my colleague PC Simon Higgins. We were wondering if we could have a word, please?'

'What's this about?'

'I'm sorry, sir, but we're investigating the suspicious death of one of your neighbours,' said Kay, keeping her tone steady. 'Liz Carter.'

'Liz? Oh... oh my goodness.' Starling moved to one side. 'Come in, please. Don't worry about taking off your shoes. We can go through to the kitchen.'

Kay wiped her feet on the coir mat then stepped inside, her shoes clattering on the laminate flooring as she shuffled to one side to let Higgins in after her.

An immediate warmth caressed her cheeks, and she unbuttoned her coat and loosened her scarf while Starling shut the door and gestured towards the back of the house.

'Beverley just put the kettle on. Would you like a hot drink?'

'No, that's kind but we won't keep you long,' said Kay, and nodded to a woman hovering beside a worktop, her grey hair bunched up on top of her head and secured with various pins.

'Love, Detective Hunter and her colleague say that Liz Carter was killed this morning,' said Wayne, moving closer to his wife and then placing a hand around her waist.

'Liz? Murdered?' Beverley's eyes widened as she raised a shaking hand to her mouth.

'We can't say for sure at the moment,' said Kay. 'We are treating her death as suspicious, though. How long have you known them?'

'About five years,' said Wayne. 'We moved here when I sold my plumbing business and took early retirement. The trees out the back weren't so big then, so we'd often stop to chat over the back fence.'

Running her eyes over a large pinewood table set to one side of the kitchen, Kay noted its surface was covered with plastic parts and paint pots.

A strong acetone smell filled the air as Beverley Starling flipped on an extractor hood above the stove top and rolled her eyes.

'I keep telling him the fumes are dangerous, but he won't listen,' she said.

Kay wandered over to the table, her interest piqued by the model aircraft taking shape. 'What are you making?'

'A Mark IX Spitfire,' said Wayne, his voice full of pride. 'I should have it finished by Christmas.'

'By which time, he's hoping the family will buy him some more kits to make in the New Year,' said his wife, her tone indulgent. 'Maybe another radio-controlled boat or something.'

'What about you, Mrs Starling – any hobbies?' said Higgins.

'Oh, just craft things. Needlework, that sort of thing. I knit blankets for the local rescue shelter.'

'Bev and I tend to call these our winter projects,' said Wayne. 'In the summer, we travel around quite a bit.'

'The camper van outside?' said Kay.

'We've been to eight different countries in it so far,' he beamed.

'Could I take a look at your back garden please?'

'Of course.' Beverley ushered her through a utility room that carried a heady aroma of cat litter, laundry powder and damp socks.

Kay passed a pair of work boots drying out on an old newspaper, water soaking into the print, and then followed the woman out into the garden.

A path ran behind the house, the crunch of gravel audible under a soft layer of snow as Kay wandered away from Beverley, leaving the woman huddled in her thick cardigan at the back door.

Beyond a landscaped terrace cluttered with an ice-filled bird bath and various seed dispensers hanging from metal stakes was a wide snow-covered lawn stretching the length of two of the neighbouring properties before it gave way to a border of thick hawthorn hedgerows and leylandii trees. A wooden shed had been built in the far left corner of the garden, with a variety of composting bins and a water butt nestled beside it.

To the right and between the branches, Kay could see the red tiled rooftop of the Carters' house.

Footprints tracked back and forth in the snow, but none went as far as the hedgerow.

'Whose are those?' she said, turning back to the house.

Higgins had emerged with Wayne Starling beside him, his gaze travelling over to where Kay pointed.

'Mine,' said Wayne. 'I was outside earlier shovelling snow off the path and put some more food out for the birds.'

'What time was that?' said Higgins, his notebook already open.

'About eight o'clock, I think.' Wayne's brow furrowed. 'Yes, eight. The news was about to start on the radio – I could hear the pips on the hour as I went out the back door with the food scraps from last night to put them in the compost bin over by the shed.'

'I-I can't believe this is happening. They're such a nice family,' said Beverley, dabbing at her eyes with her sleeve. 'The kids, too – always said hello if we bumped into them in the shop down the road or out and about.'

Wayne's mouth twisted. 'She's right. Much better than the idiot on the other side of the fence.'

'Oh?' Kay pulled out her notebook and flipped to the sketch of the crescent. 'That would be number...'

'Two,' said Wayne, 'and a pain in the backside – especially in the summer with his loud parties.'

'You can smell the marijuana from here,' Beverley

sniffed. 'I think Andrew and Liz told him to keep the music down a few times, too.'

'Did you see anyone else while you were out here earlier, Mr Starling?' said Higgins.

'No, I didn't.'

'Do you think the murderer escaped through our garden?' Beverley's eyes widened as she turned to her husband and reached out her hand. 'Oh my God. You might've been in danger.'

'It's too early to say, Mrs Starling,' said Kay. 'I'll take some photos though, if that's all right with you?'

Wayne waved her onwards, leading his wife back into the house as Higgins joined her.

'What do you think, Kay?' he said. 'First impressions?'

She bit her lip, lowered the phone and then took a deep breath.

'I don't think our killer escaped through here. There's only the one set of footprints and no sign of anyone else being here. If someone climbed over the fence and through that hedgerow or over the shed roof, I'd expect to see prints, perhaps an imprint of someone landing after a fall––'

'Right, and Starling told me the side gate has a padlock on it. I checked – no-one went through there this morning, and they didn't go over the top of the fence into the front garden from here, either – there's still snow lining the top of it. Not a smudge in sight.'

Kay narrowed her eyes as she peered at the Carters' house through the trees.

'Then how the bloody hell did he get away?'

CHAPTER THREE

'Kay – isn't that the bloke who's been on nightshift?'

Glancing up from her mobile phone, trying not to slide across the icy footpath in front of the region's media, Kay looked to where Higgins pointed to see an overweight middle-aged man easing himself out from a green four-door car parked on the driveway next door to the Carters' house.

'Let's have a word before we head back to Sharp,' she said, already marching ahead. 'Excuse me?'

The man paused, an overflowing shopping bag in one hand and a large takeout coffee cup in the other. He seemed bewildered by all the police activity in the crescent and frowned as she drew near.

'What's going on?'

Kay introduced herself and Higgins. 'And you are?'

'Ryan West. What's going on?'

'Shall we talk inside? Away from all the cameras?'

She didn't wait for a response and guided him to the front door of number two, Higgins following.

West's home held an air of neglect, as if the house was missing something – or someone.

Dust covered the top of the radiator in the hallway and clung to the paintwork between the stair balustrades, and Kay wrinkled her nose at a large patch of damp on the ceiling outside the kitchen.

'Do you live here alone, Mr West?' said Higgins as he shut the door.

The man leaned against the doorframe leading to the kitchen and shrugged. 'My wife and I split six months ago. We're trying to sell the place.'

'Mr West, we're investigating the suspicious death of your neighbour, Liz Carter, earlier this morning––'

Kay's words were cut short by West's sharp intake of breath.

'Liz? When?'

'That's what we're trying to establish, Mr West. Can you confirm where you were this morning?'

'At work.' He straightened as Higgins opened his notebook. 'You can ask them. It's the food distribution place over at Park Wood.'

'Thank you, Mr West. What time did your shift start?'

'Eight o'clock last night. I got there at half seven though, same as I always do. I like to check in with the previous shift before they leave, in case there are any problems.'

'And what do you do there?'

'I'm a forklift driver.'

'And what time did you get home?'

His eyes narrowed. 'You saw me get here.'

'Did you come home at any time before that?'

'No – why would I?'

'Any problems with your neighbours?'

'Liz and Andrew? No – never. We get on all right. They were a bit shocked when the wife left, but Andrew's good at mowing the front lawn for me if he's doing his, and I help him out with bits and pieces from time to time.'

Kay kept her gaze steady. 'And what about your neighbours at the bottom of your garden? The house in the street behind?'

He threw up his hands. 'You've been talking to the Starlings, haven't you? S'pose they told you about the parties last summer?'

'It might've been mentioned.'

'I didn't mean any harm by it. I just had a few mates around when the wife left. They wanted to try and cheer me up. We only had a few drinks. I suppose the music did get a bit loud at one point.'

'Just drinks?'

West flushed. 'Okay, one of my mates might've had a joint. I may have had a puff or two.'

'What about the other neighbours here in the crescent?'

He exhaled and dropped his hands to his sides, evidently relieved that the questioning had moved on. 'Next door at number one is fine – that's Carol. Deaf as a post, but easy to get on with. Jeff and Nicole Bernsen live over at number four. I think there might have been an altercation between Jeff and Andrew a few months ago but to be honest that's been brewing for a while – they're always arguing about the parking along here, especially now that both the Bernsens' kids have their own cars, too.'

'And number five, on the end?'

'Don't know – haven't seen either of them for a few days. Might be away or something, I suppose.'

Kay watched him for a moment, then pulled out a business card and handed it to him. 'Thanks for your time, Mr West. We'll be in touch if we have further questions. If you do think of something that might help with our enquiries, please call me at this number.'

She led the way back down the driveway, ignoring the shouted questions from the throng of journalists as Sharp and Christie emerged from the Bernsens' house, their faces grim.

'How did you two get on?' said Sharp, leading them under the crime scene tape at the end of the Carters' driveway and pausing beside the garage door.

'Apart from a complaint about loud music and recreational use of cannabis, not much to report.' Kay updated him with what the Starlings and Ryan West had told them, then jerked her chin at the house next door. 'West mentioned the Carters and the Bernsens didn't see eye to eye about the parking here. He said there was some sort of argument about it a few months ago?'

'Jeff Bernsen already told us,' said Christie. 'His kids

– Shaun and Jessica – both got their own cars in the summer, and it turned into a car park out here. Sounds like things got heated when one of the kids blocked the Carters' driveway and Andrew couldn't get out to go to work.'

'We'll check Andrew's side of the story before we leave here,' said Sharp, 'just in case there's more to it than Bernsen's version.'

Kay frowned. 'It's a long way from a parking dispute to murder though, isn't it, Sarge?'

'So is playing loud music and smoking the occasional joint.'

CHAPTER FOUR

Kay tugged her sweater sleeves over her wrists and blew on her hands as she turned away from a darkening winter sky beyond the incident room windows.

The radiator under the sill choked out warmth but did little to stem the draught from the door opening and closing with each arriving officer, and the hum of fan heaters under desks fought with the clacking of fingers on keyboards and phones ringing.

The air was thick with the smell of damp clothes drying out, and a line of woollen gloves covered the top of the radiator beside the photocopier on the opposite wall.

The team had returned from the Carters' home an hour ago leaving behind the FLO and a pair of uniformed constables to keep a stubborn media at bay.

Kay and her colleagues had spent the time since at their computers adding all the gathered statements and reports into the HOLMES2 database and following up various threads of information that would create the basis of their investigation.

She rubbed at her eyes and bit back a yawn as Higgins wandered over, two steaming mugs of tea in his hand.

'Thanks, Simon. Do you want to sit near the front?'

'Sounds good.'

DS Sharp paced the thin carpet tiles in front of the whiteboard as the team shuffled into their seats, mumbled conversations falling silent as he turned to face them, his expression determined.

'I have to report to DI Larch within the hour,' he began, 'so let's make this a productive session. With regard to the remaining neighbours in the crescent, what else have we learned since this morning?'

Higgins raised his hand. 'Sarge, I got in touch with the resident at the first house – Carol Abbott. When I went round there, another woman opened the door who introduced herself as her daughter, Grace. Mrs Abbott is partially deaf and says she spends a lot of her time sitting in an armchair next to the living room window that faces the street. She confirmed that she didn't see anyone leaving the Carters' house this morning between quarter to eight and eight-fifteen.'

Sharp's brow creased. 'Is she absolutely certain about the timing?'

'Yes, she said she was having a cup of coffee while she was waiting for Grace to arrive to help her with her shopping this morning. They confirmed it's a weekly fixture for them. They left before the first responders arrived and had no idea what happened until they got back home.'

'We've also confirmed that the neighbours at number five, the last house in the crescent, are away at the moment,' said DC Christie. 'They left for Salzburg two days ago to visit the Christmas markets, and won't be back until the weekend.'

Sharp's shoulders slumped as he turned and drew a cross through the outline of their house on the whiteboard and then repeated the action for Carol Abbott's home before tapping the pen on the outline of house number four. 'What did Andrew Carter have to say about the altercation with Jeff Bernsen and the parking?'

'He was embarrassed,' said Christie, 'and said it was something that got blown out of proportion at the time. He said he apologised to Jeff a couple of days later, and everything has been all right since. They were even talking about getting together for drinks on Christmas Eve.'

'Remind me what Andrew Carter does for a living.'

'He's an architect, Sarge.' Christie cleared his throat as he flicked through his notes. 'He's a partner in a small practice based in Sevenoaks – he and another bloke, Alan Cross, set it up six years ago and have a graduate student working for them part-time as well as a full-time admin assistant.'

'Any problems there?'

'None as far as any of them are aware when I spoke to them this afternoon,' Christie said, and turned the page.

'Liz worked as a legal secretary for a firm in Maidstone who specialise in environmental law. Again, no problems to report – and Andrew said that neither of them had received any threats.'

Sharp shoved his hands in his pockets, raised his gaze to the ceiling and exhaled before eyeing his team once more. 'All right, then – the obvious question. Did Andrew Carter kill his wife?'

Christie gestured to the whiteboard. 'Michael and Stephanie Carter confirm that their mother called out from the kitchen at eight o'clock and told them to get a move on – Stephanie said she remembers checking the time on her mobile phone. The kids also confirmed that their dad didn't come into the living room until ten past eight to use his mobile to call 999, so he's the only suspect we've got at the moment. Otherwise, how did someone get into the Carters' house, kill Liz, and leave without being seen? It's impossible.'

'There was no weapon near her body or in the house,' said Kay, 'and the CSIs have confirmed they finished their search of the garage and garden shed half an hour ago. If Andrew killed his wife, what did he do with the weapon? Both kids' statements confirm he stayed with them as soon as he found Liz until the ambulance arrived, so he didn't have time to hide it anywhere else.'

A hush descended on the room as her words sank in.

'We wait for the post mortem results,' said Sharp. 'Maybe Lucas Anderson will find something.'

'Do you think Carter poisoned her, Sarge?' Higgins

leaned forward and jerked his chin at the list of names on the board. 'Perhaps she simply hit her head when she passed out.'

'It's a good point,' said the detective sergeant, 'except that when Lucas was at the scene before you got there he reckoned the damage to her head was caused by a heavy blow rather than the fall.'

Kay chewed the end of her pen as Sharp called the briefing to a close, then wandered back to her desk as an idea began to form.

'Kay?'

She held up her hand to stop Christie interrupting and waved him to a seat beside her as she logged in to the database and typed in Ryan West's name.

Seconds later, she grinned in triumph and spun the screen around to face the older DC.

'I knew his name rang a bell,' she said. 'West was given a restraining order six months ago.'

Christie frowned as he read the text accompanying the man's photograph. 'It says here that his ex-wife filed it.'

'When uniform arrived at the scene, I don't suppose anyone noticed whether there were tread marks in the snow on his driveway?'

He frowned and pushed back his chair. 'I'll have to check. Hang on.'

Kay watched as he hurried over to a pair of constables who were headed out of the door, spoke to the male officer and then gestured for him to join them.

'Kay, this is Rob Paige – he and Lisa Nash were first on scene this morning.'

'Rob, did you notice whether there were any fresh tyre tracks in the driveway next door when you got there?'

Paige pulled out his mobile phone and scrolled through the photos. 'Here. I went outside and took a panoramic shot of the crescent while Lisa was talking to the family.'

Kay took the phone from him and exhaled before holding it up to show Christie, her heart pounding.

'There are tread marks on West's driveway. That doesn't make sense,' she said. 'It started snowing at eight o'clock last night, right?'

'Right. Where are you going with this?'

'If it didn't start snowing until he was already at work, then there shouldn't have been any tyre prints in his driveway until he got home when we saw him – they would've been covered up, wouldn't they?'

Christie's eyes narrowed. 'I think we need to have another chat with Mr West.'

CHAPTER FIVE

Kay opened the car door before Christie had applied the handbrake, her jaw set as she stalked around the front of the car and waited for him to climb out.

Fine snowflakes stuck to her hair and clung to her wool coat, obscuring the arc lights that shone over the warehouse car park and six articulated trucks parked outside loading bays.

A peacefulness enveloped the industrial park, the snow muting the sounds emanating from the low-slung brick building that housed the food distribution company.

'I'll lead this one,' Christie said, aiming the key fob over his shoulder as they hurried towards a set of open roller doors. 'Give me a signal if you notice something I don't, or if you want to jump in with a question. We'll keep this formal, but I don't want to make him nervous. According to Sharp, Andrew Carter is still a suspect, too.'

'Will do. Are you going to the post mortem in the morning?'

'Yes. Want to come?'

She grimaced. 'Only if you need me.'

'I'll let you continue going through the statements. We'll catch up when I get back if you like?'

'Sounds good, thanks.'

'Here we go.' He held up his warrant card to a man in an orange high visibility vest who emerged from a small office to the left of the doors and walked towards them. 'We're looking for Ryan West.'

'Can't he talk to you later? He's working.'

'And we're investigating a murder so it won't wait.' Christie cocked his head to one side. 'I'm sure you understand.'

The man swallowed, then pointed to where a forklift was moving back and forth between floor-to-ceiling shelves stacked with crates of tomatoes and lettuces. 'He's over there. You'll need to complete a health and safety assessment first, though – I can't have you wandering around here without it.'

'Tell you what,' said Christie, nodding towards the open office door. 'Why don't we wait in there, and you tell Ryan to join us? It'll be safer that way, and save us some time as well.'

The man exhaled before turning away.

'What if West makes a run for it?' said Kay, glancing over her shoulder as she followed Christie into the office.

'He won't get far.' Christie leaned against a wall and ran his gaze over the paperwork pinned to a corkboard beside him. 'Anyway, we know where he lives, right?'

Moments later, Ryan West entered the room wiping his hands on a rag and wearing a sullen expression.

'Mr West, take a seat.' Christie spun around the single chair in the office, the casters rattling as if about to fall off, and patted his hand on the back of it. 'Hopefully this won't take a minute.'

'I'll stand, thanks.' West flipped the rag over his shoulder and crossed his arms over his chest. 'What do you want?'

'Very well.' Christie recited the formal caution, his voice level. 'We'd like you to explain where you were last night.'

Kay heard West swallow, then stepped towards the doorway as the man's gaze shifted. 'Just tell us the truth, Ryan.'

He emitted a strangled groan, then shook his head. 'I knew I should've said something this morning. I knew it'd look worse when you found out.'

She remained silent, taking her cue from Christie as West stared at his feet for a moment.

'I forgot my asthma inhaler,' he said as his gaze lifted to hers. 'I went back home for it, that's all.'

'What time?' said Christie.

'About ten o'clock, I suppose.' West nodded towards the computer. 'Derek'll have the exact time I clocked off on there. You can check with him.'

'When did you get back here?' said Kay.

'Just after eleven.'

Christie frowned. 'It doesn't take that long to get to your house from here and back.'

'I couldn't find it when I got there. Took me a while to remember it was up in the bathroom, not where I usually leave it.'

Christie straightened and pushed the chair away as he moved to the door. 'Next time, Mr West, I'd appreciate it if you told us everything.'

'Sorry.'

As Kay followed the more experienced detective constable back to their car, she clutched her coat around her as a fresh flurry of snow scampered around her heels, and bit back a rising sense of frustration.

'Do you think he was telling the truth?' she said, launching herself at the heating controls as soon as Christie started the engine.

'Yes,' he said, 'but whether he was telling us everything remains to be seen. I still think he's hiding something from us.'

CHAPTER SIX

'Based on what you're telling me, we don't have enough evidence to arrest Ryan West at this time.'

DS Sharp pushed himself away from his perch on a desk close to the whiteboard and peered at the updating notes that Christie added in capital letters.

Kay blew across the top of her coffee and then stifled a yawn.

The incident room was quiet save for their muted conversation, the computer screens blank and only the sound of the custody suite on the ground floor filtering up the stairs to where the three of them gathered to review the case to date.

An occasional siren bleated from the street outside as a patrol vehicle swept out from the car park behind the police station, but otherwise an uneasy peace had descended on the town.

'Not at the moment,' Christie said, a note of

frustration seeping into his words, 'but he was nervous about something. We just haven't found out what yet.'

'Okay, keep your eyes and ears open,' said Sharp, turning away from the board. 'And don't be hanging around here for much longer tonight. There's another storm heading this way, and I'd rather you both got home safely.'

Christie flicked his wrist, his eyes widening as he saw the time. He swept his coat off the back of his chair, loosened his tie and jerked his thumb towards the door. 'Speaking of which, I'm a dead man if I don't get going – it's our anniversary.'

'Regards to the missus,' said Sharp over his shoulder, already heading back to his desk.

'See you tomorrow.' Kay watched the detective constable leave, then wandered over to the small kitchenette at the back of the room, rinsed out her coffee mug and left it to drain.

At her desk, she tidied the reports that had been left for her and ran her gaze across the sticky notes stuck to her screen and keyboard that jostled for space with memos requiring her urgent attention.

She wiggled her toes to encourage some circulation back into her extremities and tried to remember if there was anything in the freezer to eat when she got home.

Probably not.

Picking up a manila folder, she flipped it open and found print-outs of all the statements taken by the investigating team that morning as they worked their way around the crescent.

She found the one for house number four and rested her chin in her hand as she read through Jeff Bernsen's statement, followed by those of his adult children – all of whom were shocked by the brutal slaying of Liz Carter, despite any previous disagreements between them.

Kay flipped the page and started to read the final statement, that of Nicole Bernsen.

Then stopped.

Flicked back to the beginning and read it again.

'Sarge?'

She peered over her computer screen to where Sharp sat with his back to the wall, his jaw clenched as he read through his emails, and pushed back her chair, Nicole Bernsen's statement in her hand.

'Sarge – can I run something by you?'

He jumped at the sound of her voice, then recovered. 'I thought you'd left when Christie went.'

'Just going through some last-minute paperwork.' She held out the witness statement. 'Can you take a look at this? When you and Christie spoke to Nicole Bernsen this morning, she said that she was looking out her bedroom window at eight oh four this morning and saw Liz out on her patio holding the cat.'

Sharp took the statement from her and ran his eyes over the typed text. 'That's right. It ties in with the Carters' kids' statement that it had escaped the house and she had gone out after it.'

'How could Nicole Bernsen be so sure about the timing?'

'She said it's her morning routine to wander around

while she brushes her teeth, and that she saw the time on the alarm clock beside the bed when she turned away from the window to go back into the ensuite. Why?'

Kay sighed. 'It means the timeframe within which Liz Carter could've been murdered is even smaller than we thought...'

The detective sergeant groaned. 'Because Andrew called 999 at ten past eight.'

'Right – so how did Liz's killer get in and out of the garden in under six minutes without being seen?'

CHAPTER SEVEN

When Kay returned to the incident room the next morning, Sharp was already briefing the team about her findings from the previous night.

A few faces looked her way as she found a seat at the end of the semi-circle of chairs in front of the whiteboard and pulled out her notebook, but soon returned their attention to the detective sergeant.

She huffed her fringe from her eyes, trying to calm her heart rate after running up the stairs two at a time, cursing the traffic accident on the main road between Wateringbury and Maidstone that had created a tailback an hour long.

Save for the scratch of pens on paper, the only sound in the room was that of Sharp's voice and as she heard him recite her findings from Nicole Bernsen's statement, her cheeks flushed.

A guilt seeped into the confidence she'd felt when she left last night, an overwhelming awareness that she hadn't helped her colleagues, and only created another problem – and more work.

'How are we getting on with CCTV cameras near the bus stop on the street beyond the crescent?'

Sharp's question jolted Kay from her thoughts and she looked across as a young uniformed constable rose from his chair.

'We've received it this morning, Sarge,' he said, 'so I'll make a start as soon as the briefing's done.'

'Let me know the minute you find anything, and––' Sharp broke off and turned his attention to the back of the room. 'What is it, Maurice?'

Kay turned to see Sergeant Hoyle hovering at the door, a sheaf of paperwork in his hand.

'Thought you might want to know – I was going through the call logs from Monday night and checking them off against the system. One of our community officers was called out to Ryan West's wife's home at quarter past ten – says here he breached a restraining order.'

Kay's eyes locked with Christie's as the detective constable pushed back his chair.

'He told us he left work that night because he forgot his asthma inhaler,' he said.

'Which makes me wonder what else he might be lying about,' said Sharp. 'Best you and Kay get yourselves over there now.'

CHAPTER EIGHT

The thick snow was starting to retreat by the time Kay parked the pool vehicle next to the kerb outside Ryan West's house.

Her boots sank into a soft slush as she got out and peered over the car roof at the second house in the crescent, a weak sunlight blinking in and out of grey clouds that promised rain before the end of the day.

She shivered and hurried to join Christie as he strode towards the front door and beat his fist against the metal letterbox set into the wooden surface.

'He's probably asleep,' she murmured, gesturing to the drawn curtains across the front windows, both downstairs and at the bedrooms above.

'Hope so,' Christie said, his eyes hard.

She turned back to the door at the sound of footfalls thudding down the stairs, then a security chain rattled.

A bleary-eyed Ryan West peered out at them, a confused expression turning indignant.

'What do you want now?'

'Can we come in, Mr West?' said Christie, taking a step forward.

West moved, shifting his body to block the detective constable. 'What's this about?'

'You missed out some vital information when we spoke to you at work last night. Specifically, the fact that you lied about your whereabouts between the hours of ten and eleven o'clock.'

Christie cocked an eyebrow, waiting for the man's response.

'All right.' West moved to one side, and slammed the door the moment they both stood in the hallway. 'Come through here.'

Kay followed the two men into a spartan living room, the bookshelves bare and a lighter shade of paint on the wall where once a large television had been.

West stopped in the middle of the room and turned to face them.

'Look, I did come home to get my inhaler. I just stayed a bit longer – to calm down before I went back to work, that's all.' He exhaled and rubbed his hands down his face. 'I know I was stupid, trying to approach Ann-Marie before I came back here – I suppose it's because of the time of year – we used to love Christmas together, and now look at me.'

Kay snapped her notebook closed as Christie let out a sigh.

'Don't leave town without letting us know, Mr West,' he said. 'And keep away from your ex-wife.'

'Do you think he's telling the truth?' said Kay as her colleague closed the front door and led the way across the driveway to their vehicle at the kerb.

'About being an idiot? Yes.' Christie pulled the keys from his pocket and unlocked the car. 'As to whether that makes him capable of murder, I'm not sure.'

'What if––' Kay broke off as the front door to number three opened, and PC Alice Brooks, the Family Liaison Officer peered out and beckoned them over. 'Everything all right?'

'Mr Carter spotted you arriving,' said the FLO, 'and wondered if you could come in? He's quite anxious to speak with you both.'

'Okay.'

She followed Christie into the living room, a retro-fitted multi-fuel burning stove in the corner of the far wall creating a cocoon of warmth offset by a heavy atmosphere of grief that permeated the whole space.

A television played silently in the corner, the sports channel ignored as three faces turned to her and then Andrew Carter rose from his seat and held out his hand.

'Richard, thanks for dropping in.'

'Not at all,' said Christie, and introduced Kay to the family. 'Alice said you wanted a word?'

'Actually, it's Michael here who wanted to speak with you.' Andrew beckoned to his teenage son. 'Come on, they don't bite.'

Kay smiled at the man's gentle tone and turned her attention to the fifteen-year-old who was already the same height as his father, but who hung back with the reluctance of someone not used to being in the spotlight.

Christie's face softened as he nodded to the boy. 'It's true, we don't bite. What did you want to talk to us about, Michael?'

The teenager blushed. 'I only remembered it when Dad mentioned you were outside,' he said, his voice breaking. He cleared his throat, blinked back tears. 'It might be nothing, of course.'

'Let us worry about that,' said Christie. 'Is it something about yesterday?'

Michael nodded, then wiped his eyes with his sleeve. 'We were in here, watching the telly while we were having breakfast as usual. Dad was up in the shower. Jesse – that's the cat – he's not meant to be outside for another week but he was in the kitchen with Mum. I think she must've forgotten he was there – she's always rushing around in the mornings...' He broke off, gulped in a breath. 'There was a break in the adverts on TV – just a few seconds before the programme came back on, and that's when I heard it.'

'What did you hear?' said Andrew, placing his hand on his son's arm.

'That's the thing. I'm not sure. It sounded something like one of those hang gliders with a small engine, y'know?'

Kay frowned. 'Do you mean a microlight?'

'Yeah, that's it. Anyway, a moment later Jesse managed to get past Mum and out the back door while she was checking what the weather was doing, and then…'

The teenager turned away, burying his face into his father's chest while his shoulders heaved with sobs.

Kay turned to Christie, the confused expression in his eyes mirroring her own tumbling thoughts.

What was a microlight doing flying in this weather?

CHAPTER NINE

'Come on, I need to get something for lunch and you need to eat, too.'

Kay grinned as Higgins hovered next to her desk, her stomach rumbling as her eyes found the time displayed in the corner of her computer screen.

'Sounds like a plan.'

She locked the screen, plucked her coat off the back of her chair and followed him out of the door, squinting as a cold blast of air assaulted her face when they got outside.

'What d'you fancy?' said Higgins, leading the way across the busy main road and up the pedestrianised cobblestones of Gabriel's Hill. 'Sandwich or pie?'

'Something hot. And full of carbs.'

'You'll be moaning about that in a few months when it starts to warm up.'

'I'm willing to risk it.' She followed him into a café to

their right at the top of the hill, the windows wet with condensation and a cosy warmth inside.

Passing the smattering of wooden tables along the wall to her left, Kay made her way to the glass counter next to the till and eyed the display of hot pastries.

She picked out two sausage rolls, ordered coffee and moved to a table near the window while Higgins bought his lunch.

Beyond the glass, the pavements were crowded with office workers seeking out their lunches or running errands within their allotted one-hour break.

Sighing as she took the first bite, Kay eased back into her seat as Higgins joined her, and passed him a ketchup sachet.

'Thanks. What are you doing for Christmas this year?' he said between mouthfuls. 'Any plans?'

She wrinkled her nose. 'I've signed up to work through the holiday.'

'Seriously?'

'I figured it'd be easier than spending it with my parents.' She forced a smile. 'Besides, there's only me at home – it makes sense that I take on the shifts rather than someone with a family and kids.'

'I reckon by Boxing Day, some of those will be wishing they're at work instead.'

Kay laughed, then licked the grease from her fingers before crunching up the paper bag. While she savoured the coffee, her gaze returned to the street as a uniformed patrol passed and she held up her hand in greeting.

When she turned back, Higgins was staring into space, his chicken pie halfway to his mouth.

'Are you all right?' she said.

He blinked, then lowered the pie and leaned forward, lowering his voice.

'I think I know who killed Liz Carter.'

CHAPTER TEN

'It was us talking about Christmas that made me think of it.'

Higgins stood beside Sharp in front of the whiteboard, and tapped the enlarged map showing the crescent where the Carters lived and the neighbouring properties.

Kay sat on the edge of her seat, battening down her excitement as her colleague spoke to the gathered investigative team, his initial nerves disappearing as he warmed to his theory.

'Go on,' said Sharp.

'When Kay and I spoke to Wayne and Beverley Starling, we noticed he's an avid modeller – you know, airplanes and the like. He said he was building a Spitfire at the moment, and that if he finished it before Christmas, he was hoping their kids would buy him some more kits to work on.'

'What does that have to do with Liz Carter?' said Christie.

'His wife mentioned Wayne builds radio-controlled boats – I took a look at them while Kay was talking to his wife outside.' Higgins paused, then shuffled his feet as his face turned red. 'Anyway, I wanted to check the side gate to see if anyone had gone through there to access the Carters' garden and when he showed me through the garage to get to it, there was one of those radio-controlled drones on a workbench next to their car. It looked damaged. I just wondered if––'

'––Starling was messing about with it that morning, and lost control. Factor in the height it dropped from plus velocity, and Liz wouldn't have known what hit her,' said Sharp, his voice full of wonder.

'And it could be the case that Wayne Starling has no idea he's responsible for her death,' said Kay. 'I mean, it would've only taken seconds. If he did something with the controls, or the cold weather affected the drone's responsiveness, he might've re-established control and flown it back to his garden none the wiser.'

Sharp clapped Higgins on the shoulder. 'Good work, Simon.'

Kay nodded to her colleague as he took a seat beside her, the incident room buzzing with an excited white noise.

'Let's have some quiet and work through this,' said Sharp, his voice rising to be heard. He turned to Kay. 'What about when you were outside in the Starlings' back garden – notice anything?'

'There were a lot of footprints, Sarge, but none near the hedgerow or trees that border the Carters' garden. When I asked whose they were, Wayne Starling said they were his and that he'd been out feeding the birds and taking out food rubbish to the compost bin.' She frowned. 'He never mentioned the drone.'

'Well, according to the guidance that comes with those things, he shouldn't have been flying it out there,' said Christie. 'That's if he's got a licence for it – it's not compulsory at the moment.'

'We're going to have to be careful with this. At the moment, we have a theory but no evidence to support it – yet.' Sharp loosened his tie as his eyes met Kay's. 'Let's bring Wayne Starling in for questioning – and tell him he'll need a solicitor present.'

Kay showed Wayne Starling and his solicitor into interview room two, closed the door and crossed to the table where Sharp sat, his face impassive.

Starling and his wife were shaken by the police turning up on their doorstep, more so when Wayne was asked to attend Maidstone station for questioning.

Starling fetched the drone from his garage without a fuss, confusion in his voice as he handed it over to Higgins, who then guided him to the waiting patrol car.

Even now, when Kay glanced at the man as she entered the room, she could sense his bewilderment.

The shoebox-sized drone was now enclosed within a see-through evidence bag, which Kay placed on the table while she took her seat beside the detective sergeant and switched on the recording machine.

As Sharp cited the formal caution, she ran her gaze over the sides of the drone's plastic moulding and frowned at the scuff marks on one side, a dark substance smeared beside the right-hand landing gear.

'Mr Starling, we have some questions in relation to the events of Monday morning and the death of Liz Carter,' Sharp began. 'When my colleague DC Hunter spoke with you and asked about the footprints in the snow in your back garden, could you please confirm what you said?'

Starling cleared his throat and leaned forward, his hands in his lap. 'Of course. I went out to top up the bird feeders and empty the food scraps into the compost bin.'

'Did you do anything else out there that morning? Perhaps something you failed to mention to DC Hunter at the time?'

'I-I only didn't mention it because Beverley would've been cross,' he said. 'She's been nagging me not to fly the drone in the garden but the radio transmitter was playing up last time I took it down to the park and I spent the weekend fixing it. I just wanted to give it a quick test flight to see if it worked.'

'And did it?'

Starling nodded. 'For the first couple of minutes, yes. I got it up to about ten feet...' He broke off, frowned. 'But then the signal was lost. I don't know what happened. Bloody nuisance, to be honest.'

'What did you do next?' said Sharp.

The detective sergeant kept his hands flat on the manila folder, but Kay could sense the tension emanating from him.

She held her breath.

'Well, that's the thing. I was trying to get the drone to come back to me and land it but it went up another couple of feet, then shot across the tree line.'

Sharp flipped open the folder and pushed an aerial photograph of the area across the table. 'Could you show me on here the direction it went?'

Starling reached out. 'Here. Across the border with the Carters. Then I lost sight of it – nothing was working with the controls.'

'How long was the drone out of control?'

'Not long. Perhaps a minute. Then – I don't know – something in one of the switches gave under my touch and I could hear it again. It appeared above the trees, and I was able to fly it back. Landed it next to the kitchen door as I heard Beverley turn off the shower upstairs.'

Sharp turned the evidence bag around. 'These markings on the drone here, were they there before or after you flew it on Monday?'

'Afterwards.' Starling sighed. 'It's covered in mud or something as well – I put it out in the garage before Beverley came downstairs. I'll fix it next time she's out shopping with her friends next week. She'll be asking me what I was doing with it otherwise.'

'What time was this?'

Starling shifted in his seat. 'Just after eight o'clock, I suppose. Beverley's morning routine is like clockwork so she would've been in the bathroom at eight.'

'And so that's when you decided to sneak out and test the drone while she wasn't looking?'

'Yes.'

'Mr Starling...' Sharp paused, glancing at the man's solicitor for a moment, then back to the pensioner. 'There's no easy way to tell you this, but we have reason to believe that your drone was responsible for the death of Liz Carter on Monday morning.'

Starling paled, his eyes wide. 'That – that can't be true.'

Sharp patted the evidence bag. 'We're going to run some tests on this but believe me, I've seen enough blood in my time doing this job to recognise it when I see it, and this isn't mud. Liz Carter was killed by someone – or something – that managed to enter her garden within a six-minute timeframe and leave no footprints in thick snow. One of her children reported hearing a buzzing noise at the time, something with a small motor – such as a drone.' Sharp closed the manila folder, a sadness in his voice as he continued. 'Based on our conversation and the evidence to hand, I have to conclude that you were responsible for her death.'

Kay heard Starling's sharp intake of breath as he raised a shaking hand to his mouth.

'I didn't know I killed anyone. I didn't know I killed Liz.'

'Nevertheless, Mr Starling I am obliged to read you your rights and explain what will happen next.'

Wayne Starling held his hands to his grief-stricken face, sobs wracking his shoulders as Sharp's words rang out in the small room.

CHAPTER TWELVE

Kay filed the last of her reports to the database folder for the investigation, the satisfaction of a murder case being successfully closed tinged with a bittersweet sense of loss.

A subdued atmosphere hung in the air after Sharp explained to the investigating team that they had found their killer, a silence descending while administrative staff and uniformed officers tidied their desks, a palpable shock underlying their mumbled conversations.

It had fallen to Christie to call Beverley Starling and advise that her husband was under arrest for suspicion of killing Liz Carter, the woman's wails audible as he'd held his phone away from his ear before calming her as best he could.

Sharp had spoken to Andrew Carter, his face ashen when he returned from the family home.

'Some Christmas they're going to have,' said Higgins, his voice little more than a murmur as he packed paperwork and folders into boxes ready to be passed on to the Crown Prosecution Service in the New Year.

'Two families...' Kay shook her head. 'All because of an accident.'

'So he really had no idea?'

'None at all – Hoyle has put a suicide watch on his cell tonight, just in case.'

Higgins placed the boxes on the floor beside her desk and leaned on the topmost one. 'Are you going to be all right? You've been quiet ever since you and Sharp came back upstairs after the interview.'

'I will be.' She forced a smile, switched off her computer and pulled on her wool coat, flicking her hair over the collar. 'Safe drive home, Simon.'

'You too.'

Outside in the car park, Kay raised her gaze to the fresh flurry of snowflakes drifting in front of the streetlights beyond the security barrier, tiny prickles of ice catching on her eyelids as she inhaled the crisp air.

Her phone rang, shattering the peace.

Fishing it out from her bag, she smiled when she recognised her neighbour's name on the display.

'Jas? Everything all right?' Music played in the background, something with a piano, and she could hear the clink of glassware somewhere close by over muted conversations. 'Where are you?'

'I'm in Maidstone – Peter fancied a drink somewhere and a change of scenery. We found this lovely little bar off East Street. We thought you might like to join us, if you've finished for the day?'

'I don't know, Jasmina,' she said, a sense of panic rising in her chest as she headed towards her car. 'I wouldn't want to encroach on your date night. Besides, it's been a busy week and we've got a long day ahead of us tomorrow...'

'When was the last time you went out?' Jasmina demanded. 'I mean, out properly, not just our usual catch-up?'

'Well...'

'Exactly. Come on. Get yourself over here. Just have one, if you must. It's nearly Christmas, after all. Besides...' she lowered her voice, and Kay could hear her making her excuses as she found somewhere quieter to talk. 'There's someone I want you to meet. A friend of Peter's. I think you'll like him.'

'Jas, if you're trying to...'

'He's a vet, Kay.'

'A vet?' Kay opened the car door and slipped behind the wheel.

'You know, animals and stuff.'

'I know what a vet does, Jas.'

'He's good looking, too.'

Despite herself, despite the tiredness that crawled through her system, Kay smiled at her friend's attempts to cajole her into being more sociable and turned the key in the ignition.

'Well, in that case...'

THE END

A BURNING QUESTION

Dense smoke cast a pall across Tonbridge at seven o'clock that morning.

It stained the air, wisps tumbling on the breeze and creating a white haze over the jumbled buildings that jostled for space along the main street.

Cars slowed while suit-clad pedestrians shifted black canvas backpacks, handbags or sports holdalls from one shoulder to the other and frowned while they crossed the painted metal bridge spanning the River Medway on their way to the train station at the far end of the road.

A glow rose beyond the high street now, claiming the frigid winter's day, a portent of destruction that grew with every passing second.

For once, the commuters ignored the bird shit that clung to the railings and forgot to wrinkle their noses in disgust at the flaking paintwork, and instead wondered what was on fire.

Sirens wailed now, drawing closer, and people craned

their necks as one in time to see two fire engines tear through the junction at the far end of the road before disappearing, the roar from the engines carrying to where the bystanders gawped at each other, and then the fire-flecked horizon.

A woman in her forties, her razor-sharp tailored suit trouser hems dangling elegantly over ankle boots with three-inch spike heels, squinted through the smoke to the far reaches of the winding river and placed her hand on her companion's arm.

'Is that the boatyard?'

He looked up from his phone, shook his floppy fringe from his eyes and squinted to where she pointed. 'God, I hope not. The whole bloody lot could go up, and my sister's house is down there.'

Their pace slowed while they stared, the sound of a third set of sirens streaming towards them.

Then it was gone, dashing between the houses to reach its target.

The couple checked their watches, he shrugged and then gave her an apologetic smile.

'We'll be late.'

'We should be going.'

A cyclist zipped along the concrete path alongside the river towards the street, his luminescent lycra top at odds with the sombre weather and tainted sky. He zig-zagged between a pair of middle-aged joggers before reaching the pavement and expertly unclipped from his pedals while waiting for the pedestrian lights to change in his favour.

He caught the eye of the woman, jerked his head over his shoulder and lowered his voice conspiratorially.

'There's a boat on fire, down near the sports field.'

Her eyebrows shot upwards. 'What happened?'

The cyclist shrugged, the catastrophe already old news as he contemplated the queue outside the franchised coffee shop a couple of hundred metres away. 'Don't know. I expect it'll be online later.'

They parted ways, him resting his shoes on the pedals while he glided down the slight incline towards the café and the couple reluctantly turning away from the spectacle to hustle past the closed restaurants, determined to catch the seven-thirty service to London Bridge.

And find a seat for the journey, if they were quick.

Detective Constable Kay Hunter watched them go, then pulled up the collar of her padded coat and shoved her hands in her pockets despite the pale blue sky that penetrated the burgeoning smoke in places.

A stiff wind lifted her fringe, and she buried her lips within the soft woollen scarf that was bundled around her neck before turning at the sound of footsteps.

'Hell of a way to start a shift.'

'Hell of a way to start a morning, especially for that boat owner.' She fell into step beside DC Richard Christie, easily matching his long stride. 'How was your weekend?'

'Quiet. Not that I'm complaining. Sadie's parents had the kids over on Saturday night.' He sidestepped an older couple with a small rat-like dog with a nod of recognition, then gave Kay a rueful smile. 'We were planning on going out for a romantic dinner but by six o'clock we decided a night in front of the TV with a takeaway pizza sounded more fun. Am I officially old now?'

'Not yet. Did you ask her?'

Colour rose to his cheeks. 'I chickened out.'

'Richard…'

'I know. I will ask her. I just have to wait for the right moment, and that's not while we're watching a bad movie with lukewarm pizza.'

Kay laughed, then spotted a familiar figure a few hundred metres ahead and her good mood quickly dissipated. 'There's the guv.'

Detective Sergeant Devon Sharp held up a hand to the driver of a luxury four-by-four who braked to a standstill, then jogged across two lanes of traffic to join them, his brow furrowing when he saw Kay. 'You didn't drive?'

'In this, Sarge?' Kay snorted, indicating the nose-to-tail traffic clogging the street. 'Not likely. Besides, I only live twenty minutes away. I was on my way out the door when you called.'

'Same here.' Christie turned and led the way down a side street that curled around towards the river, then called over his shoulder. 'So, what do you think, Sarge? Have we got an arsonist on our hands?'

Sharp's face turned grim, his pace quickening. 'Three boats in six weeks? Hell of a coincidence.'

'No such thing as coincidence,' Kay murmured.

'Exactly, Hunter. Exactly.'

CHAPTER TWO

A pungent stink of rotting vegetation clung to the riverbank, redolent of autumnal debris and seasons past.

Smoke shrouded the muddy footpath that was cluttered with snaking hoses and other fire-fighting equipment, shouts carrying across to where Kay and her colleagues waited, mindful to stay out of the way until the all-clear was called.

She glanced over her shoulder to the boatyard farther along the towpath and exhaled.

At least the fire hadn't taken hold on any of the vessels lining the path at that end. The result would have been apocalyptic with the right mooring arrangements there.

Murky water rippled around the hulls of the boats beside her. There was a steady flow to the river and the level was high after the weekend's deluge while green mould clung to the paintwork of the nearest cabin cruiser, the curtains drawn and yellowing with age. An old fishing rod and a tackle box were the only items on the deck, and Kay wondered how many of the boats along here were habitable on a long-term basis.

Turning back to the source of the acrid stink swirling in the air, she saw two uniformed constables standing beside a patrol car beyond a pair of lowered steel bollards at the far end of the lane abutting the river. Their heads were bowed while they listened to a woman swaddled in a woollen blanket, one of them with a notebook in his hand.

Photographs fluttered and tumbled on the breeze as a probationary constable did her best to gather them up, and another junior officer shoved the meagre clothing that had been salvaged from the blaze into a black plastic bin liner.

'Thank god she got out,' Kay murmured. She cast her gaze over the hodgepodge of personal belongings strewn over the bank beside the smoking remains of a forty-foot narrowboat.

'So did the cat,' said Sharp, nodding at a sleek tabby that scrambled out from the blanket wrapped around the woman and landed on the soaking grass.

The cat gave the three detectives a beleaguered glare, then turned and marched off to one of the other boats moored farther downstream, where it promptly skipped on board and sat with its back to them.

'And that's why I'd always have a dog,' said Christie.

'Got a minute?'

They turned at the shout to see a senior fire officer

heading towards them, his already bulky frame ballooned by hi-vis protective clothing.

Stomping across the grass in heavy boots, he removed his helmet and ran a hand over sweat-drenched hair. Nodding to Kay and Christie, he turned his attention to the DS. 'Thought you'd want to know as soon as possible – the forensics lot will confirm it in time – but it looks like an accelerant was used.'

'Petrol?' Sharp said, craning his neck to see past the fireman to where the man's colleagues were starting to clear away the equipment.

'Certainly smells like it.' The man thrust out his hand. 'Wayne Matthews.'

'Detective Sergeant Devon Sharp.'

'So, do you think this is the same as the other fires?'

The DS pursed his lips and squinted through the hazy air as the narrowboat's skeleton emitted a sickening groan before dropping several inches into the silty riverbed. 'It's too early to say whether the three fires are connected.'

Kay turned away from the two men, gauging Sharp's cagey response.

They couldn't risk anyone alerting the media to a serial arsonist, not when their investigation was at such a critical stage.

Until this morning, when the call had come through and Sharp had scrambled his team to reach the scene of the fire, nobody in the tiny incident room at Tonbridge had ventured the suggestion that the fires were connected.

Until then, the first fire six weeks ago had been treated as a vengeance attack and the second three and a half weeks ago as an accident.

Until now…

'They'll be baying for us,' Christie muttered beside her. 'And asking why we didn't do something sooner.'

Kay glanced over her shoulder to where Sharp and Matthews were speaking in lowered voices then flapped her stiffening hands from her coat pockets and cupped her fingers to her mouth, blowing hot air across them in a vain attempt to warm up. 'Glad it's not me who's going to be dealing with the media.'

'All right, you two – we've got the all-clear.' The DS beckoned to them. 'Let's take a look, and then you can speak to the owner while I head back to the incident room.'

Following a demarcated path and lifting a fluorescent plastic tape cordoning off the immediate area beside the stricken vessel, Kay trudged behind her colleagues.

A woman in her forties stood beside the boat owner, squeezed her arm and then made her way towards them, pausing at a gate cut into a garden fence next to the towpath.

Sharp aimed a glance over his shoulder to Christie, who paused and let the detective sergeant walk on alone.

'Excuse me, did you know the victim?' Christie already had his notebook out, rummaging under his coat for a moment before extracting a plastic ballpoint pen.

The woman gave a slight nod, then wiped at her eyes.

'After everything she's been through this year, this happens.'

'Sorry, what's your name?'

'Ellie Greening.'

'What do you do?'

'Graphic design. I started up my own freelance business a couple of years ago.'

'What's the owner's name?'

'Briony Peters.'

'Does she have any family members she can stay with?' Kay asked, her chest aching as she watched the cat trot back towards its owner, its tail high.

'No. Briony and her husband divorced six years ago, and her son is currently house-sharing with two friends of his. Briony moved down from London last year because the mooring fees were getting so expensive. What with that and trying to get her yoga business established in the local area, I don't think she's had much time for making friends yet.'

'You knew her well, then?' Christie prompted.

Ellie gave him a rueful smile. 'We call ourselves "the over-40s and divorced club". I usually pop over to hers or vice versa a couple of times a week. It depends what we've got on.'

'Does she have anyone she can stay with?' said Kay.

'I was just telling her she can have my spare bedroom for as long as she needs it.' The woman peered across to where Briony was wiping at her eyes and swallowed. 'I'll look after her, don't you worry.'

Kay paused when she reached the patrol car and took a moment to look at the other houses backing onto the river.

An elderly man peered between net curtains in one of the terraced dwellings, his brow knitted together while he watched the second fire engine make its way towards the road. His mouth downturned, he gave a sad shake of his head when he saw Kay before letting the curtains drop back into place, and she made a mental note to speak to him as soon as she got a chance.

Farther along, a woman with a toddler cradled in her arms hovered behind a sturdy fence, her face pale. Kay wandered over and introduced herself.

'I thought it was going to spread,' the woman said in a shaking voice. 'I even packed a bag, just in case. You should've seen the embers in the air before the first fire engine turned up.'

'How long have you lived here, Mrs...?'

'Beckett. Joanne Beckett.' She shifted the little boy to her other hip, the child twisting his neck to see around them to watch the last of the hoses being coiled away, his face rapt. 'We moved in three years ago, from Crawley. Cormac – my other half – got a job at the hospital in Pembury.'

Kay nodded towards the boat owner. 'Do you know Briony?'

'Not really.' Joanne pulled the toddler's sweatshirt hood over his hair, then shivered. 'I've seen her around of course, and we wave if we spot each other but the boat owners tend to keep to themselves.'

'Any trouble recently?'

'Not that I'm aware of, no.'

'No raised voices or anything like that?'

The woman shook her head.

'Have you seen anyone acting suspiciously around the boats any time in the past few weeks?'

'No, sorry.' Joanne jiggled the toddler in her arms. 'This one keeps me too busy to spend time looking out the window.'

'All right, thanks.' Kay turned away and set off towards Christie, who was now talking to the boat owner.

He broke off when she approached, beckoning her closer. 'This is Briony Peters.'

'Ms Peters? I'm Detective Constable Kay Hunter.'

Briony shrugged the thick blanket up around her

neck and peered at her with baleful eyes. 'More questions?'

'Just a few, if you don't mind.'

'I've told your friends over there everything that happened.' She jerked her chin towards the patrol car that was disappearing between the houses.

'It helps us to hear it in your own words as well,' Christie explained gently. 'If that's all right?'

'I suppose so.' Her top lip curled. 'It's not like I'm going anywhere, is it?'

Kay looked beyond her colleague and spotted an old white plastic garden chair that had been tossed over the back fence of one of the properties and now lay upended amongst the weeds verging the river. She strode over, wiped it off with the sleeve of her coat, and then set it down beside Christie. 'Here, Briony – have a seat. You must be exhausted.'

'Thanks.' The woman collapsed into the chair, then wiped at her eyes at the sight of the meagre belongings being put into a cardboard box one of the neighbouring boat owners had brought over. 'Oh, God. What am I going to do?'

A sob wracked her then, and she dropped her face into her hands, her shoulders heaving.

Kay crouched beside her and dug out a tissue from her bag. 'Here. Briony, we're going to do everything we can to find who did this, I promise.'

'Have you received any threats in the past?' Christie said, his voice gruff. 'Has anyone been causing trouble down here lately?'

'A little while ago, yes. Things like door locks being tampered with, mooring ropes being cut…'

'Did you report it?' asked Kay.

Briony shot her a withering look. 'We gave up after the third time. Your lot weren't interested, and no-one even bothered to come and take statements that last time.'

Kay blushed.

'You said "the last time",' said Christie, nonplussed. 'Did the vandalism stop?'

'Until today you mean?' The woman shrugged. 'About four weeks ago. I'd got my insurance sorted out by then, thank goodness. Plenty along here don't bother, you know. They say it's too expensive.'

'What about passersby?' said Kay. 'Any trouble from those?'

Briony shrugged. 'We get the odd drunk now and again. Sometimes a group of lads will walk past after the pubs close. Rupert – he owns the cabin cruiser over there – is pretty good about reading them the riot act if they make too much noise though.'

'We'll be checking CCTV as a routine part of our investigation. Did you hear anything before your boat caught fire?'

'No. I only woke up when I heard the window break and then the smoke alarm went off.'

Kay rose to her feet and ran her gaze over the destroyed home, a deadly calm returning to the riverbank now that the fire had been subdued. 'Do you have someone to help you with this?'

'I'm insured.' Briony sniffed. 'It doesn't make up for the heirlooms and everything of course, but I'm glad I renewed it last week. Ellie's already been on the phone to them and they're sending out a salvage team with the assessor in the morning.'

Christie fished a business card from his pocket and passed it to her. 'We'll be in touch when we have an update, but if you think of anything that might help with our enquiries...'

Briony nodded. 'I will.'

He set a brisk pace back to the station, cutting through a short alleyway to a residential street running alongside the river, and Kay hurried to keep up.

When they reached the high street, he stopped suddenly and turned to her.

'You shouldn't do that.'

'What?'

'Make promises like you did back there. Telling victims you're going to find out who wronged them.' Christie took off as the pedestrian lights blinked green, slowing until she caught up. 'It doesn't always work out that way.'

'I know, but if I don't believe that, then what's the point?'

Her colleague led the way around the corner to the police station, swiped his security card and held open the door for her. 'Just remember you said that when we have to phone her to say that we've got no new leads and suspects.'

Kay watched as he took the stairs two at a time, and exhaled slowly.

'Then we just don't let that happen, do we?' she muttered.

CHAPTER FOUR

Kay dragged a spare chair with a broken wheel across the incident room, trying to ignore the pitiful squeaks from the other casters.

A small group was gathering around Detective Sergeant Devon Sharp, who in turn paced before a whiteboard strewn with coloured ink.

'Right, settle down and we'll make a start. For those of you who don't know me, I've been assigned SIO to a consolidated investigation into three suspicious fires in the area involving two narrowboats and a cabin cruiser. DC Richard Christie will deputise for me if I'm not around. Get to know each other after the briefing – we've got a lot to cover.'

Kay wriggled in her chair to offset the lack of seat padding and then craned her neck to see over the heads of two tall constables as the DS beckoned to a thin man in his mid-twenties who stood ramrod straight beside the board.

'Before we start, I'd like to introduce you to DC Blake Travis. He qualified six months ago and will be here to gain some more experience until HQ assign him to a permanent role. Kay, I'd like you to ensure he can find everything he needs while he settles in. I'm sure you'll all make him welcome.'

Travis cleared his throat. 'Thanks, Sarge. I hope to make a significant contribution to this investigation given current staffing capabilities.'

He aimed a smug look at Kay with his last words, a smirk twitching the corner of his mouth.

She felt her jaw drop, then clamped it shut as Sharp continued.

'Right, note that we're only looking at these three fires – there was another one eight weeks ago, but that has been confirmed as being caused by an electrical fault so don't let that one distract you.' The DS rapped his knuckles against the whiteboard. 'The first fire happened on a narrowboat moored down near Haysden Country Park. The owner – Jared White – says he heard glass breaking, and then the galley went up in smoke. He only got out because he smashed a chair through the window of his cabin. The fire investigator's report confirms a small petrol bomb was used, exactly the same as this morning's incident.'

Kay's pen flew across her notebook as she kept up with Sharp's commentary, her thoughts racing.

'The second arson attack took place on the other side of town, just north of Tudeley Hale, and the outcome wasn't pleasant.' The DS pointed to four photographs that showed a twisted melted hull and not much else. 'Sam Donaldson was a retired army captain with two children. Luckily they weren't on board when this happened because they live with their mother during the week, but Sam didn't stand a chance. By the time the fire crew got to him, he'd succumbed to smoke inhalation and had third degree burns.'

Sharp turned back to the group. 'Kay, I'd like you to identify the witness statements from the first two fires and re-interview those people while uniformed officers finish the house-to-house enquiries from this morning's incident. We need to establish whether there's a connection between the three arson victims or whether the person who's doing this is picking boats at random. Work with Travis on this one – I'll need Christie working through this morning's statements as they come in.'

'Will do, Sarge.'

Travis rolled his eyes, then lowered his head to his notebook before Sharp could see.

Kay bit back a sigh and continued to listen as the DS worked his way around the circle of gathered officers, issuing tasks and giving advice before dismissing them.

Christie caught up with her as the team dispersed to their desks, and grinned.

'Watch out, Hunter. Looks like our new arrival might have his eye on your job here.'

She smiled sweetly at Travis as he walked past, then glared at Christie.

'Not a chance in hell.'

CHAPTER FIVE

'I take it that you doing this means Christie's on the fast track to a promotion then, not you?'

Kay wrenched the handbrake, plucked the keys from the ignition and then glared across at Travis, who stared through the windscreen, a perpetual twist to his mouth.

'Speaking to these people might shed some light on what happened this morning,' she said patiently. 'It could be important.'

'Could be…'

He gave a slight shake of his head and opened the door, sending a gust of wind into the car that sent discarded fast food wrappers and receipts swirling in a maelstrom across the back seat.

Kay climbed out, aimed the key fob over her shoulder and followed him across a boggy path that cut through the swollen meadow leading down to the river's edge.

During the summer, this place would be teeming

with families, walking groups and avid birdwatchers but the only people she could see today were a pair of cyclists on a path in the distance, heads bowed against a ferocious headwind.

'Who are we meeting?' Travis slowed so she could catch up, his slim frame huddled within a sleek woollen coat. 'There are four boats moored along here.'

Kay pulled her flimsy anorak around her chest and shivered. 'Didn't you read the witness statements?'

'You were, so I didn't see the point. No sense in doubling up. I was reading the victims' statements instead. Quite shocking they were, too.'

'Right...' Kay eyed him sideways, then led the way across to the moorings. 'Well, first up is Neville Warwick. His boat is that large cabin cruiser on the end, *The Lancaster.*'

'Okay. What did he have to say for himself?'

'If you'd read the statements like Sharp told us to...'

Travis flapped his hand with annoyance. 'Just give me the headlines, all right?'

She paused a few metres away from the boat and lowered her voice. 'Neville was night fishing at the lake – not in the rule book, mind, so the anglers' association have banned him from doing that again – and on the way back here he says he saw someone running away from the moorings. Obviously, it was dark so he lost sight of whoever it was and was unable to give us a description apart from dark clothing and what could either be close-cropped hair or a beanie hat. Jared's boat went up in flames a couple of minutes later. If it wasn't for Jared smashing the window and Neville risking his own life to pull him out, we'd have another murder on our hands.'

Travis whistled under his breath, then peered over her shoulder at the sound of the cabin cruiser's door swinging open. 'This must be him. Shall I lead, and you can take notes?'

'I––'

But he was already striding across to the boat owner, hand outstretched. 'Neville Warwick? Detective Constable Blake Travis. I'm assisting DS Devon Sharp with the arson enquiry. I wondered if I could have a quick word.'

Kay trudged forwards, pulling her notebook from her bag as Travis stepped over the gunwale at Warwick's invitation and took a seat on the wraparound sofa that hugged the back deck.

'Detective Constable Kay Hunter,' she mumbled, nodding her thanks as the owner reached out and took her hand to guide her over.

'Is this about the fire yesterday?' he said, reaching into the top pocket of a worn denim jacket and extracting a pack of cigarettes. 'Heard someone else's boat went up in smoke. Lucky to get out, wasn't she?'

'She was indeed, Mr Warwick.' Travis cast his gaze about the river while the man lit up. 'Nice spot here.'

'Bit quieter now after the fire. It put a few of them off, and it's not tourist season yet.'

Travis swung round to face him again. 'Do you like the peace and quiet, Mr Warwick?'

The man's eyes narrowed. 'What are you implying?'

'Nothing at all.' Travis smiled, but Kay noticed it didn't reach his eyes. 'Your statement says you were returning from night fishing when Jared's boat caught fire. What time was that?'

'About two, I suppose.'

'Catch much?'

'Couple of decent sized bream.'

'Did anyone see you?'

'No, not unless whoever set fire to Jared's boat spotted me. Might be why they ran off.' Warwick tilted his head back and blew smoke into the air. 'Either that or they knew the damn thing was about to go up.'

Kay noticed the man shiver. 'Had you received any threats before the attack on your neighbour's boat?'

'There was a spate of vandalism and stuff going on for a bit. That petered out a couple of weeks before the fire. Apart from that, we're pretty much left alone here. Summer can be different but that's just normally people larking about, nothing serious.'

'Going back to the night in question,' said Travis, pausing to aim a pointed stare at Kay. 'Could you smell anything when you got closer to your neighbour's boat? Petrol, perhaps?'

Warwick frowned. 'Maybe, yes. I mean, something had to have been used to make it go up like that. Either fuel or gas, right?'

'How long was it between you getting back here and the boat catching fire?'

'No more than a couple of minutes. I lost sight of whoever it was running away, and was looking over there towards the cycle path in case they used that, but then there was this almighty sound like a clap of thunder and the front two windows of Jared's boat exploded outwards.' Warwick flicked his spent cigarette into the water, ignoring Kay's protest. 'After that, I was too busy trying to get him out of there, then moving this one so she didn't catch fire as well.'

He coughed, then turned at the sound of another man's voice.

Kay looked over her shoulder to see a man in his thirties approaching, his grey suit trousers flecked with mud and water as he traipsed across the meadow towards them.

'That'll be the bloke from the insurance company, so you'll have to push off. Jared recommended him 'cause they're paying out on his without a fight. With another fire yesterday, I figured I'd be an idiot not to.'

Travis rose to his feet. 'Thanks for your time, Mr Warwick. If you think of anything else, could you get in touch with DS Sharp?'

'That I will.'

Kay slipped her notebook away, climbed over the gunwale and walked over to intercept the insurance broker.

'Morning,' she said.

'Are you the police?'

'Routine questions, that's all.' Travis elbowed his way past her and stuck out his hand, introducing himself. 'You are...?'

'Nathan Usher. I've got a meeting with Mr Warwick at ten.' He handed Travis a business card.

'Selling insurance, eh?'

The man gave a slight shrug. 'Someone has to, right?'

'Doesn't Mr Warwick already have insurance?'

'No.' Usher waved his hand in the direction of the river. 'A lot of the people who live along here don't bother with anything other than the basic cover, thinking it's cheaper. Or they only insure for their contents, forgetting if their vessel is damaged or destroyed, often it's their homes and livelihood that goes with it.'

'Seen much business this way?'

'I've seen an increase these past few weeks, yes. What with the recent spate of vandalism and arson attacks, and nobody claiming responsibility.' Usher sighed. 'I just wish I could convince the others.'

'Right, well, we'll let you get on.'

Travis set out for the parked car, swinging his arms as Kay stumbled to keep up. 'That went well, didn't it? Plenty to think about there.'

'Uh-huh.'

'Who's next on the list then, Hunter?' He walked around to the passenger side of the car. 'You might as well drive to the next place too. I can give Sharp an update on the way. Might as well keep up the momentum, don't you think?'

'Whatever you say,' Kay muttered and threw her bag on the back seat.

CHAPTER SIX

The sun was attempting an appearance by the time Kay had driven through Tonbridge and out the other side.

She flipped down the windscreen visor before taking a narrow winding lane towards Tudeley Hale, slowing when she reached the village.

Passing a gastropub on the right, she realised it had been weeks since she had had the time to treat herself, and a smile formed on her lips as she recalled someone at the station recommending the place.

Her thoughts turned back to the investigation at the sound of a grunt from the passenger seat.

She and Travis hadn't spoken since she'd accelerated away from the country park, gritting her teeth as she listened to him informing Sharp that his interview with Neville Warwick had gone well, and that – at his suggestion no less – they were now heading towards the moorings at Porter's Lock.

He coughed. 'Who are we––'

'Meeting? The witness who phoned triple nine when Sam's boat caught fire, Michelle Chereton,' said Kay, exasperated. 'Really, you should've at least skim-read these statements to learn what's been going on.'

'I don't need to, you have. Like I said, no sense in doubling up.'

'Fine, but I'd like to lead this interview. There are a couple of questions I've got for Michelle relating to a report she filed two months ago concerning vandalism that hasn't been followed up yet.'

'Such as?'

Kay shifted down a gear, the sign for the lock flashing past Travis's window. 'Both she and Sam had windows broken, but a week after that, Sam's boat was sprayed with graffiti – hers wasn't. I'm wondering why.'

'You think someone was singling out Sam and leaving Michelle alone?'

'Maybe. I don't know yet. That's what I'd like to find out.'

'Okay, sounds like a plan.'

She relaxed then, pulling into a small gravel car park signposted for the residents of the moorings only, and running through the forthcoming interview in her mind.

Leading the way through a wooden kissing gate that separated the car park from the towpath, she spotted Michelle's brightly painted boat, *Summer Breeze* at the far end of a line of three moorings.

The first two boats she passed were deserted, almost sinking under the amount of mould and algae that clung to the hulls. She curled her lip at the smell of decay coming from them and wondered how long they'd been abandoned.

'What a dump,' Travis said, brushing past her as she paused to take a photo on her phone. 'Why anyone would want to live on a boat is beyond me.'

'It's freedom, I suppose,' said Kay. 'And the scenery always changes.'

He mumbled something under his breath, then turned at movement from Michelle's boat. 'Ah, there she is. Ms Chereton? Detective Constable Blake Travis. Got a minute to have a chat?'

Kay shook her head as he hurried towards the woman. 'Bloody cheeky bastard. He's done it again...'

By the time she caught up with him, he was chatting to Michelle amiably, admiring the small collection of potted herbs that covered the roof of her narrowboat and cooing over the fairy lights that dangled around the tiny deck.

'This is my colleague, DC Hunter,' he said as she approached. 'If you're ready, Kay, shall we make a start?'

'Ready whenever you are.' Kay already had her notebook out, choosing to stand on the towpath rather than risk squeezing onto the deck with Travis.

She might accidentally push him into the river.

'What can you tell me about the night of the fire?' Travis crossed his legs, leaning back on the plush cushions and looking for all the world like he belonged there.

'I gave a statement at the time,' said Michelle.

'Humour me. I'd like to hear it in your own words.'

'Oh. Well, I suppose it was about half-past ten when I heard a noise. At first, I didn't know what it was, but then I could smell smoke. When I opened the door, I could see flames... I keep a fire extinguisher here so I grabbed that and ran, but I couldn't get close enough to use it.' She paused and wiped her eyes. 'I could hear him inside, screaming and coughing but I...'

Kay swallowed, waiting for Travis to offer some words of comfort.

None came.

'And where was Sam's boat in relation to yours?' He twisted in his seat. 'I can't see any damage to yours.'

'He was moored at the other end, past these two.'

'In your statement, you said that your windows were broken in the weeks leading up to it,' said Travis. 'Were you being harassed at all before that?'

Kay's pen went through the thin paper, and she turned the page, swearing under her breath.

'Sam reported it at the time, actually, and someone came out to take a look,' said Michelle. She leaned against the cabin door while she stared at the deck. 'We were already patching up the windows by then the best we could, but it took forever to get all the glass out of the reeds around here. I was worried the ducks might tread on it.'

'And no-one claimed responsibility?'

Michelle straightened, then arched an eyebrow. 'Not to my knowledge. Have they?'

Kay bit back a snort at Travis's face, and instead

raised her voice. 'Are you all right out here, on your own? I mean, these two boats look abandoned, and...'

'I'm okay.' Michelle gave a shrug. 'Morris who owns the boatyard down the road has been brilliant, really. When the windows were smashed, he did us a deal for both boats to save us some money, and then when Sam's boat was vandalised again, he came down here with all the paint and helped him clean it up.' She tugged at a thread at the wrist of her thick woollen cardigan. 'He's been a godsend, especially since... since the fire.'

'How did––'

'Didn't your insurers pay for the windows to be replaced?' Travis said, ignoring the glare Kay aimed his way. 'I mean, it can't be cheap – these are specialist sizes, aren't they?'

'They are, and neither of us was insured at the time.'

'At the time?'

Michelle nodded. 'After what happened to Sam, I phoned up the broker who came to see us a week or so before the fire and told him I wanted to take out a policy straight away. I can't afford to lose my home.'

Kay heard Travis's sharp intake of breath as he leaned forward.

'What was the broker's name?' he said.

CHAPTER SEVEN

Kay sat staring at her computer screen, chin in her hand while she scrolled through the additional notes she had added to the HOLMES2 database upon her return to the incident room.

Across the room, she could hear Christie's familiar laugh as he joked with PC Lisa Nash and her colleague before the two uniformed constables said their farewells and headed out to start another shift.

He wandered past on the way back to his desk, took one look at Kay's face, and dropped into the seat beside her.

'That bad, eh?'

'That bad.'

His attention turned to her screen. 'How did you get on this morning?'

'We spoke to a couple of witnesses who were there at the time of the fires, but who also experienced vandalism to their boats at the same time as the victims of the fires.'

She leaned back and rubbed at tired eyes. 'I'm wondering whether there's a connection but I can't see it yet, and all the time Sharp has me teamed up with Travis, I'm not going to get a word in edgeways. I mean, it's bad enough that he's taking credit for my suggestions – I can live with that if it gets us a result – but his communication skills are...'

'Requiring some practice?' Christie smiled, then, seeing Travis heading their way, rose from his chair and patted her on the shoulder. 'Hang in there.'

'Yeah.'

'Richard,' Travis bellowed as he dropped his wallet and phone beside his computer keyboard. 'Any luck at your end, or still chasing leads?'

'Working on it,' replied Christie, and shot a wink at Kay before walking away.

'Well.' Travis smacked his hands together, then shot back his cuffs and logged in. 'Did you put the updates in the system, Kay?'

'I have.'

'Good stuff. Got to admit, I hate all the admin stuff. Much better when one team member takes responsibility for it all, don't you think?'

Kay bit down hard on the inside of her cheek and clicked "save". 'I think we need to widen the scope of our enquiry.'

'Oh? In what way?'

'These vandalism claims. Every one of the arson victims had their boats vandalised before the fires.'

'Weeks before the fires. There's no connection.'

'Yes, but...' She looked up as DS Sharp strode towards them.

'How are you getting on with the witnesses?' he said.

Kay straightened in her seat. 'Sarge, I think that——'

'Kay thinks that we should widen the parameters,' said Travis, cutting her off and raising his voice. 'Personally, I feel that the insurance broker, Nathan Usher, has a motive. After all, he makes more money in commission the more owners that sign up to the policies on offer. I read Briony Peters' statement last night before leaving the station, and she said that many of the owners have been reluctant to sign up because it's so expensive. They're changing their minds in droves now. There's a real sense of fear in the community because of the fires.'

Kay dug her fingernails into her palms and kept her gaze firmly on her computer screen, her jaw clenched.

'It's a very good point,' Sharp said. 'And it's certainly worth following up in the morning. What were you going to say, Kay?'

'Travis has got a fair point about the broker,' she conceded. 'But Michelle Chereton, Briony Peters and Neville Warwick told us that before the fires, there were vandalism incidents, and not all of those were reported to the police. They might have a point — so far, none of the attacks have targeted tourists, only locals. I'd like to take a look into it.'

'Waste of time,' Travis brayed. 'It's a huge step from breaking a few windows to petrol bombing someone's home.'

'But I think that——'

'Kay, if you want to follow that line of enquiry, do so. Travis, you follow up about the broker. Kay can help you with that, given you're not familiar with the area yet.' Sharp turned away. 'I'll leave you both to get on with it, but you know where I am if you need me.'

Kay watched him go, then turned back to see Travis staring at her. 'What?'

'You can look into the vandalism on your own,' he said. 'I'm not watching my career going up in smoke chasing a bad lead.'

She pushed back her chair and squared her shoulders, picked up her coffee cup and then leaned down to murmur in his ear as she passed him.

'You don't *have* a career yet, Travis.'

Kay chose to walk to Ellie Greening's house to interview Briony Peters rather than take one of the pool cars.

As she waited at the pedestrian crossing on Tonbridge High Street, the fresh nip to the air softened her temper and blew away some of the frustration and antipathy she was feeling towards Blake Travis.

She wondered whether his arrogance came from a deep-seated lack of confidence in his abilities, and then the crossing signal zapped and she recalled his laziness and reluctance to learn about the previous fires.

Shoving her hands into her pockets, she resolved to follow the lead she had suggested to Sharp, figuring that the DS wouldn't have agreed to let her pursue it if he didn't think it worthwhile.

Walking down a side street towards the boat moorings, she turned her focus to her own investigation, and the questions she wanted to ask Briony Peters.

After pausing to check her notes, she knocked on the

door of an end of terrace backing onto the river and took a step back as a figure appeared behind the frosted glass panelling.

Ellie Greening's brow furrowed when she opened the door. 'Any news?'

'Actually, I was wondering if Briony was in and whether I could ask her a few more questions.'

'She's in the living room, come on through.'

Kay followed her through a door off to the left of a narrow hallway and found herself in a comfortable space with French windows looking out to a short tidy garden. Over the back of a wooden panelled fence, she could see the playing fields beyond the river, the watercourse hidden by a line of bamboo that Ellie had planted at some point.

'Hello, Detective Hunter.' Briony uncurled herself from a large armchair, balancing a coffee mug between her hands. 'I take it there's been no progress yet.'

'We're following up some leads at the present time, but I'm afraid that's all I can say at the moment. Would you mind if I asked you some more questions?'

'Have a seat,' said Ellie, gesturing to the sofa.

Kay eyed the cat that was glaring at her from its position on one of the sofa's arms and chose a spot at the opposite end.

The cat raised its tail and sprang to the floor.

'How are you getting on, Briony?' Kay said. 'Is there anything you need?'

The woman shook her head. 'Thanks for asking, but no. Ellie's done more than enough for me, and I've already spoken to my insurers. Given the police are treating this as arson, not an accident, they don't think it'll take long for them to send me some money until the claim's processed in full.'

'That's good to hear.'

Briony's face suddenly turned stricken at the sound of a ripping noise. 'Oi, stop that!'

Kay looked down in time to see Briony's cat release its claws from the side of Ellie's sofa before it scarpered upstairs.

'God, I'm sorry, El. He's just not used to being cooped up.' Briony sighed, exasperated. 'Talk about being ungrateful.'

The other woman waved the apology away. 'It's an old sofa, and we'll get him a scratching post this afternoon.'

Kay bit back a smile, knowing the cat would probably ignore the new toy and take to carving up one of the other chairs instead before long. 'Briony, I realise this will sound like I'm asking you to repeat yourself, but it may be that you recall something today that you might've overlooked on Monday.'

'I wouldn't be surprised,' said Briony stoically. 'I've been thinking a lot about who might've done this to me, but I don't think I've annoyed anyone and I get on fine with my ex-husband now that we're living apart. Anyway, he was in Edinburgh these past four days for a conference so...'

'I'd like to go back to the vandalism you said you and

some other boat owners experienced. What happened there?'

Briony cradled her mug in her hands and leaned back against the sofa cushions. 'It felt like harassment the first time – you know, kids causing trouble. But by the second time, I wasn't the only one starting to get nervous. Rupert – the man with the cabin cruiser I told you about – got his insurance broker over because he was worried a few of us didn't have enough cover, and we lodged another report with the police.'

Kay's stomach flipped at the mention of the broker. 'Can you remember the insurance bloke's name?'

'Nathan someone-or-other. Rupert'll have his card.'

'That's okay. Thanks. Again, I can only apologise that you felt your reports weren't taken seriously at the time.' Kay lowered her gaze and pondered her next question before asking, 'What changed between the second and third vandalism attacks?'

'It seemed more targeted,' said Briony. 'The people who could afford insurance took it out, knowing that if anything more serious happened, they'd have enough of a payout to at least go to the boatyard along from here safe in the knowledge they could afford a replacement home and that all their contents were insured. We'd heard about the two fires then, and although the police weren't saying it, we couldn't help feeling that they were connected somehow. Then, when the third bout of windows being smashed happened, it was to boats like mine. Owners who hadn't taken out the new insurance policies.'

'Can I ask why you didn't?'

Briony dabbed at her eyes with the sleeve of her sweatshirt. 'I couldn't afford to. I'll get something for the boat with the policy I've got, and all my contents were insured, but I'll have to downsize. I don't want to get a mortgage at my age, you see – the banks won't lend to me anyway without a fight, because I'm self-employed. I've already had a chat with Morris at the boatyard about getting something secondhand through him,' she said, forcing a smile. 'I realised I don't need anything as big as I had, now that my grown-up kids don't visit so much, and he says he can do me a deal.'

'Is that the one along from here?' Kay asked.

'No, and Morris's yard isn't as big,' explained Ellie, 'but he's relatively new compared to them, and seems to make an effort for all the locals. I'm sure he'll have Briony back on her feet in no time.'

'What's the name of the yard?'

'Dagenham Chandlers. It's on the other side of town. Halfway between here and Porter's Lock.' Briony held up crossed fingers. 'I just have to hope the insurers pay out otherwise Ellie's going to get fed up with me taking up space.'

'Not at all.' Her friend grimaced. 'Though if you don't mind me saying, I don't think I'll miss your cat.'

CHAPTER NINE

Kay parked the pool car beside a pockmarked blue steel gate held open with a piece of thick rope, and shrugged her coat around her shoulders as she walked into the chandler's yard.

To her right, closest to the river and taking up most of the space on the expansive concrete hardstanding were eight small- to medium-sized cabin cruisers and motorboats. Each had a printed sign fixed to its prow displaying the prices, and she realised that they were all secondhand rather than the new boats that jostled for space at the larger marina in Tonbridge.

On her left was a clutch of shipping containers in various colours, well worn with rust and chipped paint hanging off their sides, and it was next to the farthest one that she spotted a man in dark blue overalls, head bowed while he aimed a welding torch to a chunky metal rod.

Not wishing to be blinded by the bright light, she

waited off to the side until the man moved and caught sight of her.

Immediately, the torch flickered out, and he raised his protective faceguard. 'Help you?'

Kay raised her warrant card. 'DC Hunter, Kent Police. Are you Morris Dagenham?'

'I am.' He paused to wipe grease-smeared hands with an even greasier rag and dropped the faceguard onto the workbench beside him. 'This about the fires?'

'And the vandalism before those.'

'Terrible business.' He gave a slight shake of his head, then beckoned to her. 'Come on in. It's warmer in the office – Louise, my wife, is here doing the book-keeping this morning so she'll have the heater going full blast knowing her.'

He wasn't wrong.

When Kay followed him into the cavernous workshop, eyeing the enormous fibreglass hull that took up most of the space, and then through to a box-like office sequestered at the back of the building, she was hit by a blast of hot air that was reminiscent of the heat emanating from the welding torch.

Morris slammed shut the door as soon as she entered. 'Best to keep it in, otherwise the costs'll go through the roof. Lou, this is Detective Hunter. She wanted to talk to us about the fires and all that.'

Kay turned her attention to the woman behind a chipped Formica table that served as the single desk in the cramped space while he moved towards an electric heater in the corner, turning down the dial before straightening.

The woman twisted her hair into a top knot, stuck a pencil through it and held out her hand. 'Louise Dagenham. Do you want a cuppa?'

'I wouldn't normally accept, but...'

'It's bloody cold, and we're having one, so don't worry about formalities for goodness sakes.' Louise was already moving towards a kettle, made small talk while it boiled, and then handed Kay a steaming mug of strong tea. 'I've put a splash of cold in it so you can drink it straight away.'

'Thanks.' Kay warmed her hands around it, her watch catching the light from a large window that took up one side of the office and looked out over the River Medway below. 'I'll bet this place is beautiful in the summer.'

'It is,' said Morris, indicating two chairs in front of the desk and sinking into one of them. 'And busy out there. Always something to look at.'

'As if you have time for that.' Louise smiled indulgently, before turning her attention to Kay. 'He's always in the workshop doing something.'

'Boats are like that, aren't they? They always need something doing to them.' Kay sipped her tea. 'I remember that from canal holidays when I was a kid.'

'Happier times?' Morris asked, noticing her reticence.

'Yeah. I don't see much of my parents these days.' Kay put down the mug. 'Anyway, sorry – I'm meant to be asking you some questions about our investigation into recent arson attacks on boat owners, as well as the murder of one of them. I understand Jared White has ordered a replacement boat from you recently?'

'God, he was so lucky his insurers paid out,' said Louise. 'Did you know we helped out Sam Donaldson after his and Michelle Chereton's boats had their windows smashed as well? The sooner you find out whoever's doing this, the better. Do you think we're safe here, in the yard?'

Her gaze travelled to the dirt-stained glass, her brow furrowing as she peered out.

'At present, I don't think you need to worry,' said Kay, 'but out of interest, what security measures do you have here?'

'The gate's locked after five o'clock at night, and that wire fence is high enough to keep out most would-be burglars. The workshop locks were changed about a year or so ago after one of them failed. We figured we might as well get the inner office one changed and the storage sheds at the same time while we had the locksmith here.' Louise turned and pointed at the computer on the corner of her husband's desk. 'And Morris set up CCTV cameras six months ago – he can view the playback here or on the laptop at home.'

'Good, okay – back to the arson attacks. Any idea who might be targeting boat owners along here? I mean, you run a busy chandlers business out of here, so I imagine you hear all sorts of things from people passing through.'

'I haven't heard anything,' said Morris. 'Although I can assure you, I'm keeping my ears open.'

Louise shot her a sardonic smile. 'You're right, people do like to gossip. So far, from what I gather, most people think it's teenagers because of the vandalism to the windows. It's the sort of thing kids do, right?'

'I sense a "but"…'

'I just can't see teenagers going as far as putting a petrol bomb through someone's window, can you? I mean, Jared said that's what was used to set his boat on fire. It's more vindictive, isn't it? Breaking windows or graffitiing someone's boat is nasty, but setting fire to someone's home? I just don't understand it.' The woman shivered despite the heat belching out from the electric fire. 'That's what scares me. If someone did get into the yard and put a petrol bomb through one of these windows, we'd lose the whole lot, just like Jared.'

'How sure are you that it was kids who vandalised the boats along from here?'

Louise shot her husband a sideways glance. 'Well, because Morris caught one of them.'

'Really?' Kay flicked through her notes. 'It's just that his neighbour didn't mention that.'

'If Sam didn't tell Michelle, there's no reason why she'd have known,' said Morris. 'When Sam told me the day after he found the graffiti what had happened to his boat, I came back here to check the recordings. Sure enough, I spotted the little bugger walking back to the boat his parents had hired on my CCTV cameras. He dumped the empty spray cans in a skip round the back of the workshop here. So me and Sam went over to the tourist moorings to have a word.' He grinned. 'I reckon the little sod's ears were ringing all the way back home.'

'What about the windows that were smashed before that? Was that the same kid?'

'No, we never found out who that was,' said Louise. 'There weren't any tourist boats around then. As it was, that particular family were only down this way on holiday because they couldn't fly to Lanzarote as planned – the kid's sister broke her leg the week before so the narrowboat holiday was plan B for them.'

'And the pair of them were miserable as anything, saying they were bored,' Morris added, shaking his head. 'I'd have loved to have done something like this when I was their age.'

Kay snapped shut her notebook. 'I think that's all the questions I've got for now, but here's my card in case you think of anything else.'

'Let us know if we can help with anything, won't you?' said Morris. 'I know it'll sound selfish given Sam lost his life only a few weeks ago, but I can't help worrying what'll happen if whoever's behind all this turns their attention to this place.'

Louise slipped her arm around him. 'Don't worry, love. It's boats that are being targeted, not boatyards.'

'I'll give you a call as soon as I've got something to share,' said Kay. 'Thanks for your time.'

She walked back to the car, tossed her bag onto the

back seat and then rummaged in her pocket as her phone vibrated.

When she read the text message from Christie, her heart sank.

Blake Travis had made an arrest.

CHAPTER TEN

Kay took the stairs up to the incident room two at a time, nearly colliding with Christie on the landing as he emerged from the third-floor door.

'Woah, steady.' He held up a hand. 'Got my message, then?'

'What happened? Where is he? Who––'

Christie wrapped his hand around her arm and led her back down a flight of stairs. 'Calm down. They're doing the interview at the moment.'

'Who is?'

Her colleague paused at the next landing, his gaze travelling to his shoes. 'Travis and Sharp.'

'Oh, for f–––'

Kay spun away from him, staring out the window that overlooked the rooftops along a cluster of side streets beyond the main thoroughfare. Her eyes stung, and her heart rammed against her ribs as she fought back anger, frustration...

'Come on. Let's go and find a quiet place to have a coffee.'

Christie gave her a gentle nudge, so she followed him out of the police station and along to a café that was almost deserted after the lunchtime trade had ended.

'We're closing in half an hour,' said the burly woman behind the counter as she swept away crumbs from the cake displays. 'And we stopped serving food an hour ago.'

'We're just after two coffees.' Christie paid and carried the drinks over to a table at the back of the café. 'Sit.'

Kay did as she was told, plucked two sugar sachets from a pot on the table and dumped the contents into her drink. 'What happened?'

'Travis interviewed Nathan Usher late last night, and apparently wasn't satisfied with the answers he got, so he went to see his manager this morning and it transpires Usher's been bringing in more work than usual lately.'

'What does that mean?' Kay took a sip of the coffee and winced as the hot liquid scorched her lips.

'Usher and his colleagues work on a commission basis, so they earn a basic salary – very basic in the case of this particular brokerage – and are expected to sign up a certain number of clients every month in order to earn more and meet their targets.'

'And I take it Usher's meeting those targets?'

'Not just meeting them – exceeding them. By a long way. His manager was really impressed with him until Travis turned up.'

'How many boat owners has he signed up since the fires then?'

'Twenty-nine.'

Kay's jaw dropped. 'All from Tonbridge?'

'No, some are from further afield, like Maidstone, but you know how word spreads in communities like that. People are scared.'

'What about alibis?'

'Brokers work alone, remotely from the office,' said Christie. 'He only has to check in once or twice a week and as long as he keeps in touch via phone or email, he and his colleagues are left alone to sign up business wherever they can. It's pretty cutthroat out there at the moment, too, from what Usher's manager told Travis. Everyone at the brokerage is worried about losing their job, and potential customers don't want to pay out for the cover because they can't afford it.'

'So Usher's been forcing the issue by vandalising boats, and when that hasn't worked he's petrol-bombed them.' Kay leaned back in her seat. 'Looks like Travis is onto something then.'

'Don't be disappointed you didn't get the breakthrough,' Christie said gently. 'Just be glad we can put a stop to the arson attacks before somebody else is killed.'

'I know.' Kay ran a hand through her hair, then smiled. 'Well, while we're out of earshot of everyone in the station, have you proposed to Sadie yet?'

'It's bedlam at home at the moment. One of the kids

is off sick from school with a streaming cold, I'm working all hours on this case at the moment...'

'Excuses, excuses.'

'Yeah, I know.' He sighed. 'I'll ask her, don't worry.'

Kay looked down as her phone pinged with a message and fished it from her bag, her smile widening.

'Is that the vet?'

Her head snapped up, heat flushing her cheeks. 'Who told you about him?'

Christie grinned. 'Might've heard something from Lisa in passing.'

Kay shook her head, unable to hide a smile. She would have a word with the uniformed constable the next time she saw her.

'Well, is it serious?'

'Maybe. I don't know yet.'

Her colleague cocked his head to one side while he watched her text a reply. 'You met him at Christmas didn't you?'

'Yes.' She tucked her phone away. 'It's just that...'

'What?'

'I don't know – we're both so busy. Him with trying to keep up with work and his studies, me doing this...'

'If it's meant to be, it'll work out. Look at me and Sadie. She works all hours at the hospital, but we manage.'

'True. Except for that marriage proposal thing.'

'Stop changing the subject.' Christie laughed, drained his coffee and stood. 'Come on. Plenty of paperwork to get through this afternoon, even if you're not leading the suspect interview.'

CHAPTER ELEVEN

The next day, Kay had arrived at work to discover that Nathan Usher had been retained in custody and that DS Sharp had applied to hold him for another twelve hours.

The questioning had gone on for most of the day but with four hours of their extended timeline remaining, rumours were swirling around the incident room that charges would be laid before long.

Now, with sodium streetlights casting a soft hue through the plastic blinds at the windows, she sat with her back to the darkened view over Tonbridge, scrolling through the statements she had processed.

After scribbling a note to remind herself to double-check when Michelle Chereton had taken out her insurance policy, she dropped her pen and looked up as Travis approached.

He bounced rather than walked towards her, grinning widely and smacking his hands together when he reached her desk.

'Well, Hunter, looks like that's one-nil to me, eh?' he said, loosening his tie. 'Are you going to buy me a drink to celebrate after we charge him?'

She crossed her arms over her chest. 'In case you missed it, someone died because of one of these fires, Travis. Two people lost their homes, and their neighbours were bloody lucky they didn't lose theirs too.'

He sobered immediately. 'Well, I... of course, of course.'

'It's not about win or lose, Travis. I do this job because I care about the people I help. Not about your point-scoring.'

'What about that drink?'

'I don't think so, do you?'

She picked up her pen once more and ignored him until he slunk away, and wondered for a fleeting moment whether he would perhaps think on her words and what responsibilities lay ahead in his role.

Then she heard his braying voice and Lisa Nash laughing with him and groaned as, one by one, her colleagues followed him out of the room.

An hour later, a piping hot Chinese takeaway to one side and a soft drink in her hand, she pored over the witness statements that she had printed out and laid across her desk.

She had spent the past two hours watching the recordings of Nathan Usher's interview with Travis and Sharp, the man becoming more agitated as the day progressed, in turn pleading with them to believe him and then refusing to disclose where he had been when fires happened.

And yet, something still niggled her.

Her phone vibrated across the desk and she snatched it up, her heart sinking as she read the new message.

Fancy a drink tonight? x

'Dammit.' She typed out a reply. *Can't, still working. Sorry x*

Exhaling, she flipped through another statement, lost in the words as she tried to piece together the missing information in Nathan Usher's answers.

'Care to share?'

She spun around at the sound of Sharp's voice to see the DS leaning against Christie's desk, his grey eyes full of worry.

'Sorry, Sarge – didn't see you there.'

He moved closer, and she held out the bag of complimentary prawn crackers.

'Don't tell anyone, I'm supposed to be on a diet and Rebecca will kill me if she finds out.'

Despite everything, Kay smiled. She had met the DS's wife once or twice at social events and had instantly built up a rapport with the woman. 'Your secret's safe with me, Sarge.'

'So,' he said between mouthfuls. 'How did you get on yesterday? I never got the chance to catch up with you.'

'The graffiti to Sam Donaldson's boat was done by a teenager on holiday. The owner of the yard at Porter's

Lock caught him on CCTV and he and Sam confronted the parents.'

'Not related to the windows being smashed along there then?'

'No. How's it going with Usher? Has he been charged yet?'

Sharp eyed her keenly. 'I've just advised Nathan Usher that he's no longer a person of interest in our investigation and that we're making arrangements to release him immediately.'

Her heart lurched.

'What happened? The way Travis was talking, it was a slam-dunk.'

The DS gave a weary smile.

'Travis may have thought he'd solved our case, but I'm afraid our latest recruit has got a steep learning curve ahead of him. Especially when it comes to doing his research properly before jumping to conclusions.'

'Oh?' Kay took a sip of soft drink. 'Why?'

'It turns out that Nathan Usher is Briony Peters' son. I just spoke with her. He's been running around trying to put together insurance deals for the local boat owners as a favour to her after she called him following the vandalism attacks.'

She snorted, sending bubbles up her nose and, spluttering, reached out for a paper handkerchief. 'Oh my god, sorry Sarge... I shouldn't laugh but... what about the celebratory drinks he organised?'

'I have a feeling he'll be drowning his sorrows instead.'

'Oh god...' She sobered. 'Why on earth didn't Nathan tell you all this in the first place?'

'He was worried it might shift blame onto his mother – apparently, she's been telling her neighbours for the past four months that she wants a new boat. He was scared that if he told us that, we might think she was responsible for the fires. As it is, Briony has solid alibis for every incident, and the fire investigation report has absolved her of any involvement in the one that destroyed her boat.'

'What a mess.'

'Indeed. Anyway – enjoy your dinner, Kay.' The DS leaned over, stealing another handful of the prawn crackers. 'And don't stay too late. I want to hear about the theory you've been working on first thing in the morning.'

'Thanks, Sarge. Will do.'

CHAPTER TWELVE

Kay rubbed at bleary eyes as she walked along Tonbridge High Street the next morning, her breath fogging in front of her.

Her alarm had gone off at five, and now she hurried towards the police station, determined to catch Sharp as soon as he arrived – and before Travis showed up.

Swiping her security card across the lock at reception, she raced up to the incident room, placed her bag under her desk, then took a moment to gather her thoughts.

She had spent the hours after Sharp left last night phoning witnesses, apologising for the late intrusion into their lives, and pulling together the final pieces of her theory until, exhausted, she had taken a taxi home, too tired to walk.

'Okay, Hunter. Make or break time,' she muttered.

Sweeping up copies of balance sheets obtained from the Companies House website, social media profiles and her notes, she crossed the room to Sharp's office.

The door was open, and as she neared she could see the DS's face illuminated by his computer screen, a stale aroma of coffee beans hanging in the air.

'Morning, Sarge. What time did you get in?'

He looked up at her voice and gestured to one of the chairs opposite his desk. 'About an hour ago.'

'It's only half six now, Sarge.'

'And what time did you leave last night?'

Kay bit her lip.

'Exactly. So, what have you got for me?'

She handed him the balance sheets. 'I think Travis was onto something when he went after Nathan Usher, but he just approached it at the wrong angle.'

Sharp raised an eyebrow. 'You're agreeing with Travis?'

'Not quite. I think if he'd been less concerned with getting a result, and more concerned with getting the *right* result, he might've come up with the same theory I have.'

'That's rather generous of you.'

'Perhaps.' She pointed at the documents in his hand. 'Morris and Louise Dagenham own a small boatyard near Porter's Lock. Until last year, they were doing okay – not making as much money as some of the bigger ones along the river, but enough to get by and live well on it.'

'What changed?'

'Morris was diagnosed with cancer nine months ago.'

'How did you find that out?'

Kay held up another page. 'Social media. His treatment was successful and he's currently in remission but it did mean that for six months, he couldn't take on any work other than basic repairs.' She leaned over and pointed at the last lines on the balance sheet. 'And their profits tumbled.'

'Go on.'

'Based on those figures and after chatting with Michelle Chereton who lives at Porter's Lock, I don't think the Dagenhams' business would have lasted much past this summer's tourist season. Except then, the vandalism started.'

'Minor repairs to tie them over the winter months, you mean?'

'That's what I'm thinking. Except there are only a finite number of boats moored along the river at this time of year, and if someone's windows are broken you're still in competition with other boatyards to do the repairs. Michelle said Morris Dagenham was the cheapest though, so she and Sam had their windows replaced by him. As did Jared and Briony.'

Sharp held up his hand. 'Wait a minute. Are you suggesting that the Dagenhams are behind these arson attacks and Sam Donaldson's murder?'

'Jared White put in an order for a new boat from them after his insurance claim was processed, and Briony Peters has said she's talking to them about a quote as well. The Dagenhams' yard provided cheaper quotes than its competitors, and probably on purpose so they can try to save the business.'

'How come you didn't ask them about all this when you interviewed them yesterday?'

'I didn't know about the boat sales, Sarge. Or the state of their accounts.'

Sharp lowered the balance sheets and stared at her. 'So if they're desperate for business, why kill Sam?'

'That's what I'd like to ask them, Sarge.'

'Get a warrant to search their premises and bring them both in for questioning, Kay.' His grey eyes sparkled. 'And you can lead the interviews with me this time.'

Morris Dagenham sat beside a harassed-looking duty solicitor and smoothed his thinning white hair across his scalp, sweat forming at his temples.

His oil-specked overalls had been replaced with a suit that hung from his slender frame, and his eyes shifted from Kay to Sharp as the DS started the recording equipment and recited the formal caution.

The duty solicitor uncapped her fountain pen and wrote the date and time at the top of her notepad, then waited for Kay to begin.

She took a moment to let the atmosphere in the room stew for a few more moments, then opened a manila folder in front of her and withdrew the copy balance sheets.

'Mr Dagenham, when I spoke to you yesterday with your wife, I asked you whether you had any idea who might be targeting boat owners with the vandalism to the windows, and subsequently the recent arson attacks that left one man dead. Is there anything you'd like to tell me before we begin?'

Confusion clouded the man's eyes. 'I, no. Like what?'

'I understand you were seriously ill last year, and that the business experienced a downturn in trade, is that correct?' Kay spun around the documents and laid them out before him. 'Quite a considerable downturn, wasn't it?

He nodded. 'My cancer treatment took over our lives for a few months. It's the busiest time of year for us usually, from June through to September. But I couldn't work – not like that. I managed to do odd jobs here and there, but we had to delve into the savings more than once.'

'You must be relieved that things are picking up again, what with all the repairs to broken windows and the like since these acts of vandalism started targeting the boating community.'

'Well, I... I suppose so. It'd be better if the attacks weren't happening at all, but if we can——'

'Take advantage?' Kay leaned back. 'Tell me about the recent order you received from Jared White.'

'Nothing to it, really. His insurers phoned him last week to say they were going to pay out his claim in full. He was lucky – he'd already passed the sixty-day period when they wouldn't have paid. So he wants me to source him a replacement boat.'

'You're not building it?'

Morris shook his head. 'As I said, those days are over

for me. I always traded in secondhand boats before I got cancer – it's useful to top up the coffers in between the bespoke work, and now it'll be one of my bigger income earners. It certainly pays more than doing repairs.'

He gave a nervous chuckle, which Kay and Sharp ignored.

Instead, Kay flicked through her notes before looking him in the eye. 'How come you caught that teenager who graffitied Sam's boat on your CCTV cameras, but nobody who might've been responsible for the windows being smashed before that?'

The man's cheeks coloured. 'Our system's been on the blink. Some sort of network glitch. I don't know why – I've been onto their technical support lot on and off for the past seven weeks trying to get a response out of them but they keep telling me the fault's at our end.'

'Are you turning off the cameras before breaking the windows?'

'What?' Morris turned to the duty solicitor, who kept a wary gaze on Kay. 'Why would I break anyone's windows?'

Kay ignored his question and instead turned to one of the witness statements on file. 'It seems to me, Mr Dagenham, that every time our victims' boats were attacked, your business stood to benefit.'

'We just provided the cheapest quote, that's all.'

'Is that all? Did you instigate the damage so that people had to come to you? Did you target people who couldn't afford the full replacement value of their homes even after an insurance payout? Did you take one look at your accounts for this year and decide you needed to take drastic steps to rescue your business?'

'No, no – that's not what happened.'

'Why burn their boats, Mr Dagenham? Their homes. Why did you kill Sam Donaldson? Did he suspect what you were doing?'

'That's not true!' Morris beat his fist on the table, making the duty solicitor jump.

She straightened her suit jacket, placed her hand on his arm, and murmured in his ear.

He sniffed, then wiped the back of his hand under his nose.

'I didn't attack those people, or their boats,' he said, eyes reddening. 'I never would, not after what I've been through this past year. I don't know why people came to us to get their boats fixed, I just do the work that's needed.'

'Then who did provide these people with quotes?'

'You'll have to speak to my wife,' he replied. 'She deals with all the marketing and accounting stuff. I just fix boats.'

CHAPTER FOURTEEN

Two hours later, Louise Dagenham turned away from the duty solicitor appointed to her when Kay and Sharp walked into interview room three and took their seats.

The man beside her handed over business cards, then spoke his name for the recording once Sharp had made the introductions and read out the formal caution.

'Why am I here?' Louise asked. 'Where's Morris? What's going on?'

'Mrs Dagenham, I'd like to ask you some questions,' Kay began. 'As DS Sharp has indicated, this is a formal interview.'

'Okay, but––'

'When I visited your boatyard yesterday, both you and your husband told me that you had no idea who might be involved in the vandalism and arson attacks on local boat owners. I also understand from speaking with several witnesses to the three fires that have occurred in the past six weeks that you've shown a keen interest in the owners and neighbouring vessels, even before the fires happened.' Kay looked up from her notes. 'In fact, you've been in close contact with boat owners at each location for months. Why?'

'Well, whoever's doing this could target us next, couldn't they? I was just trying to find out what was going on. Your lot weren't doing anything. I mean, what would happen if whoever's doing this decides it's not enough to petrol bomb a boat and attacks our boatyard instead?'

'I think that highly unlikely, Mrs Dagenham.' Kay took an evidence bag from Sharp, noticing the slight nod he gave her. She broke open the seal with a flourish. 'Do you recognise this?'

Louise's mouth turned into an "o" of shock. 'Where did you get that?'

'From your office at the boatyard. You'll recall that when I arrived there with my uniformed colleagues this morning I informed you that we had a warrant to search the premises.' Kay opened the accounting ledger. 'Is this your writing, Mrs Dagenham?'

'How did you get that? It's kept in the safe...'

'Your husband was good enough to give us the combination code an hour ago. Is this your writing?'

Louise paled. 'Yes.'

'Unusual for a business these days to keep manual records. Doesn't your accountant prefer you to use an online system?'

'We do.'

'Then why have this as well?'

'It's... it's just the way I prefer to do things. As a back-up, in case the system fails.'

'So, if I get a warrant to demand your accountant hand over a copy of your current online transactions, this book will match those will it?'

Louise said nothing.

'Or,' Kay continued, 'will I find some extracurricular activities recorded in this that your accountant – and the taxman – are unaware of? Like the cash that was also found in the safe. All fifteen thousand pounds of it.'

'Look, maybe one or two minor jobs, that's all.' Louise turned to the duty solicitor. 'Everyone does that now and again, don't they?'

'I spoke to Jared White before I walked in here,' said Kay. 'He confirms that he never spoke to Morris after his boat was vandalised, and in fact, it was you who approached him. He said you were most insistent that he didn't give the work to one of the larger boatyards, and that you told him they were turning away work because they were too busy.'

'I was just trying to be neighbourly.'

'He doesn't live anywhere near Porter's Lock.'

'It's a community though, isn't it? All these boat people. They like to stick together.'

'They do indeed, Mrs Dagenham. Did you provide the quote to Jared after his boat was destroyed in the fire?'

'Yes.'

'I understand you visited Jared at his daughter's house where he was staying and doorstepped him into accepting it.' Kay watched as the woman's jaw clenched. 'He said he felt guilty, especially after you explained about Morris's illness.'

'I was just trying to help.'

'Who?'

'Morris. Us.'

Kay closed the ledger and folded her hands on the hardback cover. 'Louise, it's time to tell the truth. This has gone too far. Did you deliberately vandalise boats to ensure a steady stream of work for your boatyard?'

'No comment,' Louise murmured.

'Did you – when it transpired that the income from repairs wasn't enough – then escalate to arson, and petrol bomb Jared White's boat so you could secure a finder's fee for a replacement?'

'No comment.'

Kay handed the ledger back to Sharp and watched as he re-sealed the evidence bag and added his signature. She took a deep breath before asking her next question.

'Mrs Dagenham... Louise... Why did you murder Sam Donaldson? Was it because he refused to have his windows replaced by Morris? Was it revenge?'

Louise blinked. 'How did you know we didn't fix his windows?'

'Our witness recalled that although Sam got a quote from you, he ended up having them replaced by another supplier – one based in Maidstone. Is that why you killed him? Did rage get the better of you?'

'No...' Louise's face crumpled. 'He wasn't meant to die.'

A shocked silence followed her words, and Kay could almost hear the whirring of the recording equipment under the sound of the woman's sobs.

'What happened, Louise?'

'He was meant to escape like Jared did. I didn't know he was sleeping on the sofa in the main cabin, not the bedroom.'

Kay bit back bile. 'You threw the petrol bomb into the living area, didn't you?'

The woman nodded.

'Why didn't you go back and try to rescue him?'

'What was the point? It was too late for him. The flames were too much, and the smoke...' Louise raised her gaze and sniffed. 'I felt so stupid. I'd just lost us a sale.'

CHAPTER FIFTEEN

'Bloody hell, she's a cold one.'

Christie squinted against a low sun and held up his hand to a passing patrol car as he walked beside Kay along the main street.

They had left the station together, Sharp's congratulatory speech still echoing in Kay's ears, and her spirits lifted by Blake Travis being the first to shake her hand.

'I owe you an apology,' he'd said.

'Accepted.' She'd smiled, and tipped her can of beer against his before mingling with the rest of her colleagues.

Now, she huffed her fringe from her eyes and loosened her scarf.

There was a warmth to the air this evening, a promise of spring finally on the breeze, and she inhaled deeply as they crossed the River Medway. Farther along the watercourse, a cabin cruiser slowly floated out of the town's reaches and towards the country park, its passengers clutching wine glasses and their laughter carrying back to where she stood.

'So, I take it her husband didn't have a clue what she was up to?' Christie paused a few paces away, waiting.

'No.' She caught up with him and snorted. 'I don't know whether it was naïvety on his part or whether his whole focus was on his health, but he was shocked when we showed him the ledger – and the footage Lisa Nash subsequently found of Louise leaving the scene of Briony's boat after she set it alight. Travis managed to obtain CCTV footage from a convenience store down the road from the moorings that shows Louise getting into her car. She really did think she'd got away with it.'

'Again.' He stood to one side to let an elderly man on a mobility scooter pass, then shot her a bashful look. 'Sadie's parents had the kids over last night, so we had the place to ourselves. I didn't get a chance to tell you earlier.'

Casting a sideways glance at him, Kay noted the faint smile on his lips. 'Well? How did it go, then? Did you ask her?'

'I did.'

'And?'

His smile widened, and she gave him a playful punch on the arm.

'Spill it, Christie. Do I have to buy a new dress or what?'

'She said yes.' His voice held a note of wonder. 'Sadie said yes.'

Kay whooped, gave the taller detective a brief hug,

and set off once more. 'Congratulations. Although can I just say, I told you she would?'

'I know.' The smile was still in his voice. 'The kids were happy too when we told them this morning. Mind you, I think in Charlotte's case, that's just because she gets to invite her best friend. Or perhaps choose the flowers for the bridesmaids' bouquet. Hard to tell with a six-year-old sometimes. Oh, by the way – I overheard Sharp on the phone before we left. Sounds like the recruitment freeze is going to be lifted for a few months. That means new opportunities.'

'Oh.'

'You don't sound too happy about it.'

'New opportunities sometimes means moving on, doesn't it?'

'Maidstone calling, perhaps? You've helped with a few cases based out of there before, haven't you?'

'I don't know...'

'You'll see. Don't underestimate yourself, Kay. It'd be a good move for you.'

'But I like it here.' She heard the panic in her voice. 'I like working with all of you.'

'Don't worry – it might not be for a while.' He smiled. 'After all, there's a few people in line for promotion ahead of us at the moment anyway. But I'll bet they ask you one day.'

'Maybe.' Kay jerked her chin towards a side street. 'Okay, this is me. See you in the morning?'

'Seven fifteen on the dot. According to Sharp, he

wants a full debrief at eight so we'll pick up some decent coffee on the way in if you like.'

'Sounds good. See you.'

Despite the anticipation of having to relocate, Kay took a moment to reflect on the past week and the result the team had got. She would never accept it as her win, not with the amount of manpower it took to collate all the witness statements and carry out the searches – and the work wasn't over yet.

But for now, there was a lightness to her step and she hummed under her breath as she realised there was a decent bottle of chardonnay waiting in the refrigerator at home.

She stopped when she turned the corner into the road where she lived.

Parked outside her block of flats was a scruffy, mud-clad four-by-four.

Standing next to it was a man with dark curly hair dressed in jeans and a suit jacket, and he was smiling at her.

'Adam,' she said, hurrying over. 'I'm so sorry – I know I was meant to call you back, but we had a breakthrough, and...'

He grinned and pulled her into a hug before kissing her. 'I heard. Well done.'

'Thank you. Who––'

'Someone called Lisa Nash told me when I phoned to speak to you. You'd already left though.'

'Lisa... She's such a gossip.'

'In the best possible sense.' He kissed her nose. 'Fancy a celebratory dinner tonight?'

'Sounds like a great idea.' Kay grinned. 'And I've heard about a really good gastro pub not too far away from here.'

THE END

ABOUT THE AUTHOR

Rachel Amphlett is a USA Today bestselling author of crime fiction and spy thrillers, many of which have been translated worldwide.

Her novels are available in eBook, print, and audiobook formats from libraries and retailers as well as her website shop.

A keen traveller, Rachel has both Australian and British citizenship.

Find out more about Rachel's books at: www.rachelamphlett.com.